SHIKHANDIN is a writer based in India.

IMMODERATE
MEN

Stories

Shikhandin

SPEAKING
TIGER

For Kallol Biswas

SPEAKING TIGER PUBLISHING PVT. LTD
4381/4, Ansari Road, Daryaganj,
New Delhi–110002, India

First published in India by Speaking Tiger in paperback 2017

ISBN: 978-93-86582-10-2
eISBN: 978-93-86338-45-7

10 9 8 7 6 5 4 3 2 1

Typeset in Minion Pro by SÜRYA, New Delhi
Printed at Thomson Press India Ltd.

Contents

Banquet for the
Son-in-law

Shasti Babu chewed on a guava twig and contemplated his banana tree. The tip of the twig had become a brush after two minutes between his teeth. He spat out loose fibre and massaged his teeth and gums. The banana tree grew at a slant on the tiny patch of land adjoining his back door, and almost tipped over into Nani Gopal's house. Shasti Babu knew his next-door neighbours stole a leaf or two every now and then, so he kept a watchful eye on his precious tree. Especially now that a glossy garnet-coloured banana blossom was curving out of the foliage and Jamai Shasti was only a month away.

Shasti Babu's daughter had been married off the previous year with as much pomp as he could muster. He prayed that his daughter's in-laws were pleased with all that he had given them—his daughter, the ten grams of gold jewellery she wore on her wedding day, the twenty Tangail saris as namaskaris, the top-class plywood bedroom set, the Salem steel utensil set, the six-kilo rohu fish, the boxes of extra-large sweets for the totto, the Bajaj scooter, the Titan watch and gold buttons for his son-in-law, as well as the guest house where he had put up all forty of them for three days. The wedding had been the talk of their locality.

Nani Gopal's wife, whose own daughter had not had such a grand wedding, had come to them complaining that her daughter-in-law had not brought half the things Shasti Babu had given his daughter. She had then added with a glint in her eyes, 'But my daughter-in-law is so fair, naturally her parents didn't have to work hard at finding a boy.' Shasti Babu ignored the jibe, but Bimala fumed and gnashed her teeth for days. 'We will see what colour grandchild she gets! Mark my words, it will be coal-black like her son. Or striped, like a zebra!'

Shasti Babu's concerns, however, were of a more immediate nature—what to feed his son-in-law for Jamai Shasti. For, as Shasti Babu well knew, the onus of keeping his daughter's in-laws happy by showing his eternal gratitude towards them for having selected her fell squarely upon his shoulders.

Sundari, the cow, rubbed her neck against the banana tree. 'Ai! Hut-tut-tut!' Shasti Babu charged towards her with his arm raised. Sundari flicked her tail at him disdainfully and moved away. 'Arrogant cow,' muttered Shasti Babu under his breath as he shortened the rope with which Sundari was tied up. He didn't want her upset.

Sundari was a good cow. A cross between a Patnaiya and a New Zealand breed, she was as beautiful as her name implied. She had brought two female calves into the world after joining Shasti Babu's household five years earlier. One of them had already fetched a good price. The younger calf remained by her mother's side, drinking the three litres of milk that Shasti Babu generously allowed it from the thirteen litres which Sundari generally produced. Now that the calf had started to eat fodder, he was seriously thinking of reducing her quota by a litre. Good quality cow's milk sold for fifteen rupees a litre. Sundari was an important earning member of the Shasti household.

Shasti Babu inspected the banana tree one last time before going inside. Bimala met him at the kitchen door and handed over the two cloth bags he needed for the market before going back into the kitchen. She would get the rice and dal done by the time he returned with their day's requirement of vegetables and fish. Shasti Babu had retired from his post as a non-teaching staff at the local college. But he still went there and kept the ledgers on a freelance basis. The money was a pittance, but it gave him something to do, and helped him stick to his earlier routine for at least part of the day. It also kept him out of Bimala's hair in the morning, so her own routine was not disrupted. Shasti Babu enjoyed a breakfast of rice with dal and fritters or some light fish gravy before leaving for college.

With the bags rolled up under his arm, Shasti Babu went up to Sundari. Every day he took the cow and the calf to Gobindo's cowshed. Gobindo milked Sundari and measured out the milk under Shasti Babu's watchful eyes. The calf mooed in anticipation of the moment when it would be let loose and allowed to rush at Sundari's teats. Gobindo paid Shasti Babu twelve rupees a litre for the milk. That was three rupees less than the market price, in lieu of which he took Sundari and her calf out to graze along with his cows. Gobindo brought her back in the evening, when he milked her again under Shasti Babu's supervision before the latter took Sundari and her calf back home. What Shasti Babu did not know was that Gobindo milked her in the afternoon as well, and extracted two litres. Ignorance is bliss. Shasti Babu amiably listened to Gobindo gossip as he milked Sundari, and she flicked her tail at both of them.

Shasti Babu counted the money. Today Gobindo had given him less than usual. But he was not worried. The amount due would be jotted down in Gobindo's hisheber-khaata, and repaid when it was time to sell off the second calf. Gobindo would either buy the heifer himself or act as a go-between for its purchase by a fellow milkman. He would also deduct the fees for the services of the stud bull that he kept, and which had impregnated Sundari. This was the standing arrangement he had with Shasti Babu and other bhadrolok Bengalis like him who owned a cow or two, but would not or could not make a business out of the animals.

Shasti Babu, content with the money in his pocket, walked off to the haat to buy their daily necessities. He was by nature a contented man. Even when he prayed for his daughter's happiness at her in-law's, he prayed with the sort of satisfied half-heartedness that told Bholanath, his patron lord, that Shasti could adjust his degree of contentment according to the lord's dole.

Shasti Babu first scoured the market, looking for bargains. Today's prized catch were the small carp swimming around in earthen pots. But the koi or climbing perch which looked like they were of the correct breed, and would do Bimala's cooking justice, were a tempting choice, too. Shasti Babu, whose expert eyes could make out the pedigree of any fish, ogled the koi eagerly. Of course it would not do to let that thug Jiban Das know how eager he was, for that would make him lose his bargaining power. He acted extra gruff, but the koi was too much to resist and he did not clinch the deal entirely to his satisfaction. Shasti Babu consoled himself with the thought that sometimes quality mattered more than price, and moved on to the vegetable sellers.

The season for cauliflowers had waned, and those that were still around were ragged things that even Sundari would reject. The cabbages had already lost their winter crispness. However, the pumpkins looked bright, and the tomatoes were smooth and red, though less juicy than their sisters in season. The saving grace of the market was the mound of potol or wax gourds lying on a jute mat before the vendor. Shasti Babu looked at them and visualized the dolmas Bimala could make for Jamai Shasti.

Lately, Shasti Babu had taken to visualizing every vegetable and fish for the banquet for his son-in-law. Every time he encountered a particularly robust ash gourd, or a tender long bottle gourd, or an irresistibly succulent prawn, he would close his eyes and see it in its most splendid culinary form. In this happy mood of anticipative reverie, Shasti Babu had of late been buying more food than was necessary for his wife and himself, much to Bimala's vexation. Today was no different, and by the time Shasti Babu was through, his pockets were empty and his two cloth bags were bursting at the seams.

Bimala received his bounty in silence. She knew he was going through the initial process of selection through elimination for that perfect meal, the memory of which would carry their daughter through the rest of the year in sheer marital bliss. She had been cooking two extra items for the past three weeks to work out possible choices for the final menu. Later, after their siesta, when she served cups of tea with Marie biscuits, both of them would discuss the pros and cons of the dishes tried out that day and the night before. The menu would be drawn up afresh every time an item appealed but did not match with the rest. This problem of a constantly changing menu was compounded by another matter. They did not know much about their son-in-law's food preferences, except for two things. First, he liked fish more than mutton, but was allergic to shellfish. And second, he loved sweets but not the standard shop-made rossogollahs and pantuahs but the complicated home-made variety, like gokul pithey, paatishapta pithey, chhaanaar jilepi and so on.

Their son-in-law's sweet tooth created a bit of a problem for Bimala, because the season for good date jaggery had ended, and most of the sweets he liked could only blossom under the influence of that fragrant brown sweetening agent. Shasti Babu was generous with advice but Bimala knew she had to come up with not just a reasonably good substitute, but one considerably superior to the original. Beads of sweat would gather on her forehead as she grated the coconut for yet another version of gokul pithey.

~

The days flew by as Bimala sweated it out in her kitchen. Shasti Babu put on a couple of kilos. Summer gathered steam and the menu changed one more time. Meanwhile, the banana blossom grew and grew until it almost touched the ground. Shasti Babu could tell what delectable mochaar-paturi it would make. He watched its growth excitedly and, two days before Jamai Shasti, he brought Bimala out in the early hours of the day to take a look at the culinary prize growing in their garden.

The banana blossom was gone.

Bimala and Shasti Babu stared at the blossom-less stub in disbelief. A solitary outer petal lay on the ground where the vandalism had taken place. The hoof mark on the powdery surface of the dry soil clearly revealed the culprit's signature in the pale morning light. Sundari must have somehow come loose in the night. Shasti Babu angrily stalked off. Bimala sighed and went back inside to make their morning tea.

Sundari's frantic mooing brought Bimala rushing out. Also Nani Gopal, his wife, son and daughter-in-law. Nobody had seen Shasti Babu lose his temper like that before. Nobody had heard him shout so loudly or beat Sundari either. Sundari ran frantically about, her tail lifted high, and her distressed calf mooed miserably as it strained at the rope. The Nani Gopals enjoyed the show for a full half-an-hour before Shasti Babu sat down on the steps, panting and clasping his hand to his heaving chest. Bimala quickly ran inside to get him some much-needed water and a haath-pakha to cool his forehead.

'Shasti-da, running so hard at your age is not good for your heart,' admonished Nani Gopal.

'How would you feel if you were vandalized by your own family member?' gasped Shasti Babu, still clutching his heart.

'What has happened has happened. You will have to find a substitute dish now,' said Nani Gopal's wife, smiling slyly.

Bimala looked at her sharply. 'How did you know what we were going to do with the banana blossom?'

'Wasn't it obvious? Why would Shasti-da check on it every day? Poor Sundari. I don't think she will give any milk today after that beating!'

'You're right. Sundari should not have been beaten. Who knows who the real thief is?'

Bimala went quickly inside before Nani Gopal and his wife could react. Shasti Babu also got up and limped indoors after tying Sundari up. Nani Gopal's wife's shrill voice trailed after him into the house, provoking them to a fight. But Shasti Babu was too disheartened to take up the challenge, and Bimala refused to give her the satisfaction.

They drank their tea in morose silence. Bimala handed him the two cloth bags silently and he took them without cheer. Shasti Babu went out and untied Sundari to lead her to Gobindo. Sundari followed quietly, though distrustfully, her muzzled calf ambling close. The day had begun badly. Shasti Babu was in no mood to exchange pleasantries. So when Gobindo failed to extract milk from Sundari, he, already put out by Shasti Babu's mood, gruffly enquired what was wrong with the cow. Shasti Babu didn't reply. And, instead of leaving Sundari with Gobindo, he brought her back home and un-muzzled the calf. The calf, amazed by this sudden generosity, rushed at her mother's udders and started punching at her teats with her mouth.

'O go, forget the haat today,' said Bimala, fanning her husband gently with the haath-paakha. 'There are already so many vegetables in the house. You go take your bath and I'll get the meal ready.'

Shasti Babu looked at her with stricken eyes and nodded. Bimala looked at him as went inside and her eyes filled with sudden tears. They had both grown old. It was not fair that he had to endure such stress after retirement. They had done their duty and got their daughter married. Now it was their turn to go off on that long postponed pilgrimage to Hardwar and Kaashi, to enjoy their siestas unfettered by visions of their daughter's displeased in-laws. She wiped her hands on the edge of her cotton sari and went into the kitchen.

Bimala poured rice starch from the boiling vessel into a pail. The warm gruel was Sundari's treat and seeing her eagerly drink it made Bimala happy. She took the pail and went out to Sundari. She found the cow staring at Noni Gopal's maid, who was washing vessels. The maid was muttering under her breath as she scrubbed hard to rid a large pot of sticky bits of boiled banana blossom. Sundari heard Bimala's footsteps and turned to look at her with large reproachful eyes. Bimala blew a kiss at her and softly coaxed her to come near.

'Now be a good girl and drink. I'll give you some sweet bananas afterwards. As for this disgusting theft, Sundari, we'll keep what we've discovered to ourselves. We don't want Shasti Babu to get a heart attack, do we?' Bimala stroked Sundari's neck and crooned into her ears.

Sundari relented after a while and bent down to drink the gruel. Bimala went back into the kitchen for the promised sweet bananas and gave both Sundari and her calf a few; quickly, before Shasti Babu could find out. Shasti Babu, ignorant of this latest development, ate a little before leaving for work. Bimala soaked the dishes for the maid to clean and went off for a bath. The house was silent except for the steady scraping sound made by the jhanta as the maid swept the house. Bathed and fresh, Bimala sat in her puja room for her hour of bliss and peace. But today was not the day. The maid ran into her pristine puja room in her stale clothes, shrieking with excitement.

'O Ma, O Ma, come and see this!'

Bimala scowled, but got up as curiosity got the better of piety. They both went out. Sundari was standing still, with milk dribbling from three of her teats, while her calf suckled furiously. Bimala stared. Sundari chewed cud nonchalantly.

'Quickly! Run and get Gobindo. Now! Hurry!' Bimala almost pushed the maid out. Then she spent the next frustrating minutes watching the milk flow uncollected. The maid returned with Gobindo. Bimala produced a pail and set the fellow to work.

'There are hardly six or seven litres of milk here,' said Gobindo. 'The calf has polished off most of it and the rest has dribbled away! I have told Shasti-da so many times to keep that calf tied up. Chhi. What a waste! I left my cows in the field for this!'

'Gobindo, this milk is enough for me. Thank you for milking Sundari, I won't forget this favour,' said Bimala as she took the pail inside.

Gobindo went away, grumbling to himself. The maid went back to her chores. But Bimala did not restart her prayers. Instead, she took out a handful of batasha from the jar kept in her puja room and held it out to Sundari. Sundari took this offering without batting her eyes, but she did not flick her tail at Bimala either.

Shasti Babu returned from work and quietly ate lunch. He took his customary paan after the meal and retired into the bedroom. For the first time in weeks, they did not discuss the banquet. Bimala fanned him as he lay on his side and pretended to sleep. She felt bad, but did not say anything to comfort him. Shasti Babu's retirement had taken more of a toll on her than it had on him.

Bimala had prepared many elaborate meals in her time, as a young bride and as the mother of a young girl who was shown to almost as many grooms as the twenty-two years she had spent on this earth. Bimala's mother-in-law had believed in ruling her son's home with an iron hand. Bimala and her co-sister had suffered quietly, drying their tears on the edges of each other's saris, until a day arrived when the younger woman quarrelled bitterly with her mother-in-law and left with her husband and small son in tow. After that the burden of her mother-in-law's strictures had fallen entirely on Bimala's shoulders. But she had taken it all in her stride, without ever complaining to Shasti Babu. Bimala had been brought up in the old school, where the mother-in-law was to be obeyed, though not necessarily loved. Bimala had tried to impart these values to her only child, though her motherly instincts had made her gentle. She had also filled the girl's ears with warnings and admonitions as she filled up the wedding trays. But her responsibilities hadn't yet ended. Their jamai had to be fed and fed well, at least once every year. Bimala spat red paan juice into a spittoon, took up an old copy of *Desh* and read for a while before falling asleep.

Dusk was already creeping in when Bimala woke up. She found Shasti Babu twitching his feet on his favourite perch, a threadbare cane chair he had inherited from his father. She quickly went into the kitchen to make their evening tea.

'What are we to do tomorrow, Bimo?' said Shasti Babu in a voice that nearly broke her heart. 'Just a day left to prepare for Jamai Shasti. I should have finished the shopping today; tomorrow it will be so crowded and expensive.'

'You've taken too much of tension today. Just relax. One banana blossom gone isn't the end of the world. Haven't I been trained by your own mother? I will manage very well, don't worry. Our first Jamai Shasti. You think I will let my own daughter down? Or even let the neighbours have fun at our expense?'

'You do what you think best, Bimo. After all this is your territory.'

They drank their tea in silence, watching the sun slowly slip away.

Bimala didn't go to bed till long after Shasti Babu had started to snore fitfully. She was too excited to be sleepy. Besides, she had rested well in the afternoon. The quiet night gave her space to work in her 'territory'. Like Sudhir Moira at the nearby sweetshop, Bimala worked long into the night to greet the new day with batches of freshly made milk sweets. She had already boiled and portioned off the milk that morning—so much for the paneer, so much for the kheer and so much for the rabri. Bimala toiled with a calm energy until the whole house smelled sweet and the sweetness entered Shasti Babu's dreams. The birds had begun to utter their first

notes when Bimala finally finished. She tidied up the
kitchen and put the sweets in the meat-safe in her puja
room, where she normally kept the bhog for Lakshmi
Puja and the Sottonarayon Puja. She still had a couple
of hours left before the day's bustle started. Bimala lay
down beside Shasti Babu and immediately fell into a
deep dreamless sleep.

'Wake up Bimo, I made you tea.' Shasti gently shook
his wife.

'What time is it?' she asked.

'A little late by your standards.' Shasti Babu smiled.
'Looks like you didn't sleep well. Yesterday's episode has
bothered you much more than me. Don't worry about
Jamai Shasti. We are what we are, and have done what we
could for our daughter. Now it's up to Bholanath.' Shasti
Babu raised his hands as he invoked the lord's name.

Bimala said nothing. She bent her head to tie her hair
into a knot and quietly took the cup. Shasti Babu liked to
surprise her sometimes with morning tea. Usually after
they had had an argument the night before, or when
Bimala was sick, or when Shasti Babu wanted to show
affection without appearing to be hen-pecked.

Shasti Babu went out into the garden. Sundari was
still wary, but his cajoling voice and the proffered
bananas soon put her at ease. He was honestly sorry
for having beaten her, and spent a good ten minutes
explaining why he had been angry, stroking her as he

spoke. Sundari listened to him without flicking her tail, breathing moistly into his face. Shasti Babu left for the haat shortly afterwards, whistling a tune as he passed Nani Gopal's house, with Sundari and her calf walking beside him. He was determined to be happy and not let the steep pre-Jamai Shasti prices in the haat spoil his mood.

The haat was more crowded than usual, with people jostling for the choicest vegetables, fruits, fish and meat. It had a festive air about it, and everyone who entered the haat couldn't but be affected by it. Swept up by the tide around him, Shasti Babu jostled and bargained and made his purse stretch as best he could. Nani Gopal brushed past him with two bulging bags, plus a servant boy carrying another two behind him. They exchanged greetings, and if Shasti Babu noticed the smug look on Nani Gopal's face when he glanced at Shasti Babu's meagre purchases, he didn't show it.

~

Shasti Babu had taken leave from work. He needed one day for the preparation and the next for the actual celebrations. So today, after a light breakfast, he would sit down with Bimala, a cup of tea beside him, ostensibly to help her wash and clean the fish and vegetables, but mostly to be there with her as she worked. It gave him a nice Sunday feeling, having a second or third cup of tea on the verandah in front of the kitchen, with Bimala sitting at her bonthi with the vegetables spilled all around her, the whole scene bathed in soft morning sunlight. Shasti Babu poured some tea into his saucer and appreciatively sucked in the tea.

Bimala smiled. 'You did manage to get the potols to go with the fish-peti, didn't you?'

'How could I not? After all, who makes potoler dolma like you? Our Jamai will remember the taste till his dying day!'

'Balai shaat! Balai shaat! How can you say such an inauspicious thing?'

'Mistake, mistake.' Shasti Babu grinned. Then his face became a little serious. 'Bimo, do you think all this is enough for a good meal?'

Bimala looked at her husband. The lines on his good-natured face seemed freshly drawn. His hand trembled a little as he lifted the saucer up to his lips.

'There is something I wanted to show you. Actually I wanted to surprise you, but you are so worried...' Bimala got up and motioned him to follow. Shasti Babu put down his cup, a puzzled frown on his face.

'See these? I made them last night. You think our Jamai won't remember this feast? He will. I guarantee. But first, just to make sure, I want you to taste each and every one.'

Shasti Babu stared at the treasures his wife displayed

in her meat-safe. It was packed with brass plates, each covered with the lace doilies she had tatted years ago as a young woman, plates that were loaded with sweets. His eyes moist with emotion, Shasti Babu stared as his wife placed a serving of each on a steel plate.

'O go, we have done all that we could for our child. Now the rest is our Bholanath's responsibility. Come now, and eat. I know how much you love these sweets,' said Bimala, her voice husky with emotion. She sat Shasti Babu down and started to feed him her creations. 'Who else do I really cook for, if not for you?'

'You will have to give me company Bimo,' said Shasti Babu in a trembling voice. 'I am not so young anymore.'

Shasti Babu and Bimala sat down together there among the scattered things for the banquet, laughing and weeping at the same time; they sat sampling the sweets, each tenderly feeding the other. The sun lingered above them that morning, peeping over their shoulders, unwilling to leave their little nest.

Room Full of Presents

Priti looked over the letter once more. She had read it three times already that morning, and yet she felt she had to, one more time, just to make sure. The letter had arrived from Messrs Dastidar & Ray, who had sent it 'on behalf of the Late Devnath Gupta, and in accordance with his express instructions'. The solicitors had advised her to be present at their office on the fourth of February at 10 a.m. for the reading of Devnath Gupta's will.

Priti needed to discuss this strange event in her otherwise very uneventful and proper life with Trina, her daughter.

Trina was sensible and calm, a natural leader, though she had a mulish streak that once used to bother Priti. But not anymore. These days she was happy to let Trina take the lead. She dialled Trina's office.

'What is it, Ma?' Trina's voice was clipped and self-assured. A third person might even consider it rude, but Priti knew better.

'There's this letter, Trinu. From Dev's lawyers.'

There was a pause.

'Dev who?'

'What do you mean who? You know which Dev I'm talking about. He's dead, did you know that?'

'Yeah. I think I read his obituary somewhere, but didn't give it much thought. He used to be your batchmate, right Ma?'

'Yes. Now this letter...'

'What does the letter say?'

'Um… I've been asked to see his lawyers the week after next. Something about a will… I don't know why...'

'Ma, I'll see that letter on my way back home, okay? Don't worry, I don't think there's anything to be afraid about. Unless you've been up to some hanky-panky after Baba died!'

'Trinu! That's a horrible thing to say. What do you mean I…?'

'Oh Ma! Can't you take a bit of teasing? C'mon now, don't be such a prude! All the girls in your batch had a crush on him! Including you! That didn't stop Baba from loving you the way he did, or you him for that matter! You stay put. I'll drop in early, okay?'

Priti smiled as she replaced the receiver on the cradle. Trina's teasing made her feel more at ease. The letter had startled her much more than she would admit. Yes, it was true that she'd had a crush on Dev. But so had all the other girls in her class. And, if her suspicions were true, some of the lady teachers had also been a little bit in love with him!

Dev had been the stuff of a Mills & Boon romance. He was good-looking, and extremely rich. To make matters worse, he had also been an excellent student. So nobody could say that it was his father's money that had bought him a seat in Calcutta's most prestigious college. Dev could have gone abroad to study if he'd wanted to. Instead, he'd chosen to finish college in dusty, crumbling Calcutta. Of course, unlike the other girls and boys in his class, he hadn't opted for a master's degree in the same subject he had studied for the bachelor's. Nor did he sit for the bank and civil service examinations like many did. Instead, he had opted to study management in one of the most premier institutes in the country.

Priti still remembered the day he drove into college in a sleek red car of foreign make. That was more than thirty years ago, when anything foreign still drew oohs and aahs from hoi polloi. He had worn a short kurta, blue jeans and Kohlapuri chappals—considered the height of fashion in her time, and which had come back a full circle now. Except that women preferred it more nowadays than men did, she thought ruefully. Trina always wore jeans with loose khadi kurtas.

In college Dev would always be surrounded by a bevy of beauties. He was no less popular with the guys, though. Together, Dev and his friends formed a charmed circle of the beautiful, the wealthy and the fashionable. Priti was not a part of that circle.

What circle had she been a part of? After all these years, Priti still didn't know. She used to be pretty, in a petite, girl-next-door kind of way. Most took her reserve for shyness. She hung out more with girls than with boys, and was serious about academics. Her professors had always liked her. Her girlfriends had teased her about Dev, but only mildly. Their womanly intuition had zeroed in on something a little out of the ordinary in the way Dev's glances fell upon Priti. But Priti was a closed book. Her classmates expected her to have an arranged marriage. She smiled now as she thought of her college days. Love was not something you rushed headlong into, she had always felt. It was a little seed you nurtured in a pot, waiting for the right elements for it to sprout. During their college days she had seen the callow romances of her batchmates. Yes, Dev had made her feel shy and feminine, and also desired. But so what? Everybody was attracted to him, and he seemed to be available to everyone. Her instincts told her to stay aloof, but not so remote that his attraction for her dried up entirely. Good Bengali girls did that; they never humiliated their admirers or stamped a little seedling to death. They would often share the same bench in the classroom, and the scent of his cologne would warm her cheek, but Priti would seek refuge in an open book.

Once Dev had offered her a lift as she walked to the bus stop after class. It was summer and she could feel perspiration running down her salwar-clad legs. She had looked up, half inclined to say yes, and found herself staring straight into three pairs of eyes reflecting alarm and hostility. They were girls from another department, all three of them seated in the back seat. The passenger seat next to Dev was occupied by a boy from their class.

'No thank you,' she had replied coldly. 'Your car is already full.'

Dev had nodded, not looking at her, smiling tightly. He had never offered her a lift again. Her refusal had given her minor celebrity status among her friends and classmates for a while. And even afterwards, she sensed their respect. Dev continued to be polite towards her. But they remained on amiable terms, greeting each other as old friends do, whenever they chanced to meet again at some classmate's wedding or the other.

Priti had finished college with good marks; good enough to find her a place in Columbia University. She met Samaresh there, in her sophomore year; he was finishing a doctorate in sociology. They became friends, discovered shared interests, and gradually fell in love. They both returned to Calcutta, because it never occurred to either of them not to. After that, marriage, a university lectureship, Trina's birth, several years spent being a committed mother to Trina and wife to one of the most respected academics of Calcutta University, and then back to teaching again.

Altogether, Priti's life had been uneventfully happy. Devnath Gupta made an occasional appearance in her social circuit—far removed from his flamboyant and sometimes scandalous life—as a subject for gossip at dinners and get-togethers. Priti had remained in touch with most of her schoolmates. Samaresh had a larger group of friends from his school, college and university. And they, along with their spouses, made up Priti's circle of close friends. Whenever conversation would flag, one had to merely mention Dev's name and at least half-an-hour's worth of animated and sometimes heated conversation would be assured. Of course, Priti would always have some anecdote or the other about his escapades in college to relate, while the rest of her group would keep her updated on the most current gossip about him.

They would make catty remarks about Dev's women—his current mistress or wife. The husbands would mostly hover silently around them holding their drinks. And the conversation would invariably end with one of the men remarking, sometimes with ill-concealed sarcasm, to his wife, 'Aren't you lucky to be married to a boring fellow like me?' If his wife felt up to it she would say something in jest; someone else would crack a joke or steer the conversation elsewhere. Priti and Samaresh would look on, and then at each other. Dev had been discussed early on in their relationship, when the first confidences were shared. Priti knew about Samaresh's crushes, including the one he had on his cousin sister. They were both living so far away from familiar people and places at that time that the intimacies they built, their mutual confessions, and the lessons learnt among strangers had made them comrades and lovers.

Of course Samaresh had met Dev, several times. Usually at one of the Dover Lane musical nights or at a theatre. And Dev had been as polite and charming as ever. A little distant though. Perhaps because of his position as a business magnate, an industrialist who hobnobbed with politicians, movie stars and other industrialists. Priti hadn't expected him not to be conscious of his wealth and status, but she had been a little rankled each time by the way in which he would look over her quickly and speak only to Samaresh. She had fumed a little about it once, but Samaresh had only laughed and teased her. Samaresh would often tease her about Dev, sometimes in front of Trina. In fact, Dev was a bit of a private family joke, and even a mention of his name would bring out impish grins on the father's and daughter's faces.

Now both Samaresh and Dev were gone. Samaresh had had a cardiac arrest more than three years ago and

Priti had never quite recovered from his death. And Dev had died in a car accident.

~

'Ma, this is just a letter asking you to be present at the reading out of his will,' said Trina. She had come as promised and was now sitting with her legs stretched out at the dining table. She held the letter in front of her, squinting at it. 'There's nothing to worry about. He was known as a generous man. Maybe he's left all his college mates something; including you!' This last bit was delivered with her trademark grin.

'But that'd be so silly,' said, Priti frowning.

'Why?' demanded Trina, and Priti had no answer.

'Ma,' said Trina, putting a friendly and undaughterly arm around Priti's still slim shoulders. 'Ma, you didn't have anything to do with him, I mean in terms of business, etc. You're not related to him. The only relationship you had with him goes back to your college days. And people can be pretty sentimental about their ol' mates y'know. I can't think why his lawyers would have called you unless he wanted to give something to you. His will probably mentions some little something to be given to everybody he knew from his student days.'

Priti looked at Trina. 'You'll be there with me, won't you Trinu?'

'Of course!'

~

The young man who ushered in a very nervous Priti and a slightly nonplussed Trina had been very respectful. He turned out to be one of Samaresh's ex-students.

'You won't remember me, Mrs Mukherji, err, ma'am. But I had gone to your house once to get some notes from Sir,' he said, standing in front of her and tilting a little forward, duck fashion. 'Won't you please go inside? Both of you.'

He opened a stout mahogany door and ushered them into a small office. Priti was glad to sit somewhere private. She had noticed the unfriendly looks a couple of ladies waiting in the main hall had flung in her direction. These women seemed to be of the same age as her, but were dressed in the height of fashion. There were some young people, too.

'Those are his ex-wives,' whispered Trina in her ear. Then frowning to jog her memory, she muttered, 'I thought he had married four times? Nah! The other two were mistresses! Ma, your ol' mate was some womanizer!'

'Trinu! Do be quiet. The poor man is dead and here you are gossiping!'

'Oops! Sorry!' Trina said with a grin. 'Anyway, no one heard me so it's okay.'

The man had left discreetly. He must have instructed someone to send in refreshments because, soon afterwards, a uniformed bearer entered the little room with a tray. The bearer respectfully set down two glasses of chilled water, two cups of steaming coffee and a plate of cream biscuits.

'That's nice,' said Trina, reaching for the cup of coffee. 'Ma?'

Priti shook her head. She still didn't feel quite comfortable in Dev's solicitor's office. Trina looked at her keenly for a second or two, then shrugged and took a long sip. Priti sat up straight in her chair, looking at but not really seeing the mahogany bookcases lining the walls, packed with rows of formidable leather-bound books.

The man returned after what seemed, at least to Priti, a very long time. This time he was not alone. A bald man with silver side-locks was with him.

'Ma'am,' he said to Priti, still tilting duck fashion in spite of Trina's irrepressible grin, 'this is Mr Dastidar, our senior partner. Sir, Mrs Mukherji.'

'Namaskar, Mrs Mukherji,' said Mr Dastidar kindly. 'We are sorry to drag you into this, but Mr Devnath Gupta expressly wanted you to have the gifts.'

'I'm afraid I don't understand,' said Priti, visibly flustered.

Trina put a protective arm on Priti's shoulder. 'Can you tell us how this... I mean the gift business, came about?' Trina looked at Mr Dastidar directly. 'Ma and he were just classmates, you know. We weren't expecting...'

Mr Dastidar raised a palm, smiling. 'We understand perfectly well how you feel. I know this is very awkward for you ma'am, but we have to follow our client's instructions. I can assure you of complete discretion and privacy. In fact, even Devnath Babu's current wife is not aware that he has left you anything.'

'Why would he want to leave my mother anything?'

Mr Dastidar paused for thought before clearing his throat to speak again. 'Devnath Gupta was a very curious man. He was a public person who had a very private side. Mrs Mukherji, he was a very unhappy man, despite everything that he had. To tell you the truth, he had, especially during his last years, before that very sudden accident, begun to rely more on us than even on his children. He didn't seem to be able to trust anybody. Not his family, not his friends. His death is still under investigation. His assets, which are very considerable, will be held in trust till the whole thing is cleared up.'

'In that case, how come Ma gets these gifts or whatever...' said Trina interrupting him again.

Mr Dastidar smiled at Trina gently. 'These so-called gifts don't come under his assets. As I said, he was a very curious man. These are personal items. He used to collect them every year. He asked us to keep them for him a couple of years before his... err... this tragedy. We were instructed to hand them over to you if he died before you, and destroy them if you departed before him. He had a notebook, a diary of sorts, in which he used to make entries on certain dates, Mrs Mukherji. He used to buy the gifts for specific dates or occasions…' Mr Dastidar looked directly at Priti. 'Those dates concern you, ma'am, I think. Here it is,' he said, handing Priti a sealed brown paper package.

Priti took the package silently, almost fearfully. It contained Devnath's diary. Trina was not the only one who sensed her discomfort. Mr Dastidar and his junior looked at her kindly. Their faces seemed to say that they understood how she felt. Priti was glad, but it didn't lessen the awkwardness. Not a bit. She was very quiet on the way home. Trina, sensing her mood, didn't try her patience with her usual lighthearted remarks and jokes.

~

Trina brought her seven-year-old son along later that evening. 'We are sleeping over,' she said airily to Priti as she walked in.

The solicitors had sent over a vanload of parcels that same afternoon after Priti had formally taken receipt of them. Trina had helped unload and dump the presents, for that was exactly what they had turned out to be, in the guest bedroom. The presents were in all shapes and sizes, beautifully wrapped and tied with silk ribbons. They covered the queen-sized bed, the study table, the dressing table and the floor in-between, in a double layer. The room looked festive, like one in a bride's house.

Priti looked at them apprehensively, not daring to enter, while Trina instructed the two men who had brought in the load. 'For the time being,' she had explained to the bewildered Priti. 'You can sift through them and browse at your convenience without cluttering up the whole house.'

The men had left shortly afterwards, as had Trina, after promising to return in the evening. 'The wrapping papers will fetch quite a bit from the bikriwalla,' she'd quipped, but Priti hadn't smiled.

Priti sat down in the arm–chair in her drawing room, holding Devnath's diary. And she stayed like that until Trina returned in the evening. The diary sat like a stone, waiting to be turned over and reveal what lay underneath.

'Ma,' remonstrated Trina. 'You're really very troublesome! Couldn't you get yourself a cup of tea at least? Did you eat anything? What's wrong with you Ma, c'mon!' This last bit was accompanied by a clumsy hug.

Priti looked up at Trina and drew Binku close. The child, as if sensing that his grandmother was disturbed, had crept near and was looking up at her with big brown eyes instead of running around the drawing room like he usually did.

'I was waiting for you, Trinu. Didn't feel like doing anything for myself today.'

'Hm! Binku, you look after Dida while I go rustle up some food for us.'

Priti picked the boy up and hugged him. She smelled Binku's baby odour and it calmed her. She had been feeling a little light-headed ever since the letter had arrived, and the feeling had become worse after the visit to the solicitors'.

Priti hadn't wanted to open Devnath's diary. Not yet. She was curious, yet afraid of it. A part of her didn't want to know. Why had he accumulated presents for her? And why her, of all people? The questions swam round and round inside her head, skirting the answer that waited patiently to be revealed. She was too old for this sort of thing. She felt she had betrayed Samaresh in some way. She wished he were here now. The wish grew into an ache. She wanted Samaresh here with her, only Samaresh and no one else. Priti clutched Binku tightly. The child wriggled in her lap.

Trina came in after a while and forced her to sit with them at the dining table. 'Okay. If you don't feel like eating, I won't force you. But at least give me some company and feed Binku. Ma, won't you?'

Feeding Binku was a ritual that involved telling him stories. Priti didn't feel up to it, but she led him to the table. She knew the effort of story-telling would keep her mind away from the jumble of thoughts that was threatening her placid life. And that diary, waiting quietly on the side table.

~

She went back to it right after she had fed Binku and eaten a little herself. Trina came in and sat next to her later, after Binku had gone to sleep.

'Would you like to take a look, Ma?' she asked in a quiet voice.

Priti nodded and stood up. She picked up the diary and beckoned Trina. They went into the guest room together.

'I'll pick up a present at random and read out the date on the tag,' said Trina. 'You can check the entry on the diary for that day. Okay Ma?'

Priti nodded. Trina held up a package wrapped in shimmering silver paper. She opened it carefully, trying not to tear the wrapping.

'Fifth July—your birthday, Ma,' said Trina. '1978. That's simply ages and ages ago!'

Priti opened the diary and leafed through the pages. She read the entry under that date:

'My Priti, my very own and very precious Priti. I had this little brass figurine specially commissioned for you. If you look underneath, you'll find your name etched on it. I hope you like it. I know you love little Ganesh murtis. So I had this made, just one piece. One unique piece, for my one in a million Priti…'

'Ma, it really does have your name underneath!' Trina held up the little Ganesh figurine for her to see. 'You know who made it? Goshto Kumar! Imagine!'

Priti took it absently. Trina didn't seem to have realized the strangeness of the words her mother had just read out. Or perhaps she actually had, but didn't want to blurt out her opinion, like she normally did with Priti.

Priti put the figurine down and started to read at random. Page after page, entry after entry, said the same thing, in different words, describing different gifts but referring to the same set of dates. It made no sense. Not at first. The dates swam before her like a school of sardines that had lost its collective sense of direction beneath the shadow of a trawler. Then, like a flash, the numbers tallying with Trina's birthday rose up, and the rest fell into place soon after.

Priti put the diary down. Her hand flew to her mouth and she choked down a cry. The dates that had meant so much to Priti—her's and Trina's birthdays, her graduation day, her wedding day, her anniversaries, the day Samaresh bought their trusty Ambassador—every single date that held even a smidgeon of importance had been swallowed up by Dev. He had claimed each date for his own, annulled the people dearest to her and directly associated with the dates, and replaced them with himself and a child of his own. The diary contained an imagined world, a blissfully happy imagined world, inhabited by real people—Priti, Devnath and Trina. The realization chilled Priti. For a few maddening moments her own life seemed unreal, as if she had just awoken from amnesia.

What had Dev done? What had he been doing with his life? And why? She hadn't known. How could she have known? She loved Samaresh. Not Dev. But her heart knocked against her ribs. And Samaresh wasn't there to reassure her. The diary mocked her. It mocked her life with Samaresh. It was as if Dev had sucked him out like the marrow from a curried goat shank. And there was nothing left but a long hollow through which she could see only emptiness beyond.

'Samaresh', whispered Priti. 'Samaresh'. His name a shibboleth on her lips, Priti tried to clear the mist from her mind. She let the diary drop on to her lap, and her forehead slumped against the palm of her hand.

Trina, who had stopped opening the presents by now, watched Priti with concern. She then quietly took the diary from Priti's unresisting hands and began to read from it. The words began to blur as Trina, who usually never had any patience with emotions, began to weep silently. Priti got up and sat down next to Trina. Her cheeks were wet, too. And soon after, as Trina held her tightly, Priti's shoulders convulsed with soundless sobs. She wept; wept for having broken a man's heart that she had never meant to break; wept because she couldn't have helped it, even if she had known. She wept and wept as the night quietly wore on, around her and Trina, and around the ghosts that trod softly past them towards their place of final rest.

Stolen Spoons

The afternoon spills its mellow light on the bald patch growing slyly on Manish's head. He quickly walks over the short distance from the car park to his apartment block. He's home early, early enough for his work-day to be counted as a half holiday.

'It's the spoon,' he mutters to himself as he presses the lift button.

The spoon is a heavy white-metal piece with an ornate stem. Manish can't tell for sure why he pocketed it at the lunch he was sharing with his colleagues. He had wondered, as he rinsed his mouth in the restroom, how his colleagues would have reacted if they knew. Then he had shrugged. What did those boring sods know about him anyway? He had felt an urge to be with Rupa as he returned to the table, and excused himself as soon as he decently could.

He wonders what Rupa will say, and smiles to himself. The first time he'd stolen a spoon was also the first time they had met. Right after they had become engaged.

They had gone to a restaurant together, chaperoned by Rupa's elderly aunts and a gaggle of cousins, mostly girls. Mercifully, the chaperones had taken a separate table.

He remembers how uncomfortable they had both been. How neither of them had been able to say anything at all. Manish had tried, but the giggles wafting towards them, the heat from the many pairs of eyes, had stopped him. Rupa had been too nervous to do anything other than twist the embroidered corner of her sari-end. Acting on impulse, Manish had picked up a spoon and whispered to her to reach under the table. When the cool metal touched her fingers, Rupa's eyes had widened. A smile had lit up her face and deepened the dimples on her cheeks. The next time they met, her eyes had sparkled with anticipation when he reached for a spoon. By the time they were married, she had collected a dozen spoons.

When was the last time I brought home a spoon? Thinking this, Manish pauses at the door.

Rupa and he have been together for many years. She is still attractive enough, he thinks, in spite of the two pregnancies and the hysterectomy. Manish himself has a just few more years to go before retirement. He still hasn't made any post-retirement plans; he still feels young and energetic. And today especially so.

Three, sometimes four times a week, Manish has sex with Rupa. Safe, uncomplicated sex, delivered silently, and just as silently received. He is happy with the arrangement, glad to be free of 'tension' when he's at work. On the days when Rupa fails to deliver, he eases himself in the privacy of his bathroom, before his morning shower.

Usually, Manish is never home before seven o'clock, by which time it has grown quite dark. Rupa has finished her evening prayers, and the house is smoky from the agarbattis at the altar and the mosquito-repellent coils burning in the corners of rooms. Dinner is ready and waiting, just for the two of them, now that their daughter has moved abroad. He washes up and changes into a loose shirt and shorts as soon as he comes home. He switches on the television in the living room—the same channels every day. Rupa hands him a cup of tea with two biscuits on a plate. She shares this evening ritual with him. Afterwards, Manish makes some work-related phone calls, reads a business paper or magazine and watches some more TV. Rupa busies herself with clearing away the table and making preparations for the following day's breakfast. When they retreat into their bedroom, she switches off the lights before removing her clothes. She gets into bed where Manish awaits. In the shadowy room, Manish tries, but never manages to catch Rupa's eye.

They'd had their share of adventures before the children were born. They'd tried out different positions illustrated in the books he brought home. Once they even had sex in the balcony of a hotel room. But after their first child died within a few months of birth, Rupa grew aloof. The loss of a son, their scion and heir, had hit all their family members. Manish does not have too many clear memories from that phase; he mostly remembers Rupa's coldness, the time it took for her to return his embraces, his feeling of helplessness and even outrage, for it was their entire family's tragedy, not just hers alone. Several years had passed before Rupa could become a mother again. But the second pregnancy resulted in a daughter. And then the baby claimed so much of Rupa's time and attention that Manish had wondered if he would have to go elsewhere. But he had never expressed his displeasure openly. And the idea of using force disgusted him.

Today, his normal orderly life is not itself. Today is exciting, even unnerving, and arousing. Manish turns the door key. The breathy silence in the house tells him that Rupa is probably taking a nap. He glances at his watch. It is a little past three in the afternoon—her regular time for a siesta, one he shares with her on Saturdays, Sundays and other holidays. Manish hesitates. Should he enter the bedroom quietly and lie down beside her, after placing the spoon between them? Should he just leave the spoon next to her and return to their living room to wait? Or should he simply wake her up?

Manish removes his shoes as quietly as possible. He puts his laptop down gently on the sofa instead of going into the study and dropping it on his table like he usually does. He tiptoes towards the dining table and places the spoon next to the salt and pepper shakers. The cool marble floor sends up light tingles through his feet. Manish inches his way towards the partly open door of their bedroom. He pushes it a little and then a little more, with infinite care. The bed with Rupa on it swings slowly into view. Manish leans forwards and stands still, too shocked to even blink.

Rupa's eyes are closed, her mouth is half-open. She is moaning softly, and her legs are sliding up and down the smooth surface of the bed even as a busy hand slips in and out of view. She is alone, but she may as well have lain there with a lover, someone with whom she is so much at ease with that the scars on her belly, its folds and bulges, the railway map of veins on expanded skin, far from making her feel shy, can be flaunted with abandon. Her hair, which had once been long and silky, is now a mess of slate-coloured locks spread out on the pillow. Manish backs out into the living room as quietly as he had entered. He sits at the dining table, fingering the spoon.

What should he do now? Should he go in and tell her to stop, and behave herself? Should he join her? He feels himself, but the little fellow is quiet, as timid as a mouse trapped between his thighs. The idea of Rupa behaving like that is preposterous. But there she is, in the next room, wallowing in her private, marshy world. Should he slap her and then have sex with her? The last thought startles him, and just as quickly shames him.

Manish puts his head in his hands. Is she dissatisfied with him? Has he given her reasons to stop loving him? Is she in love with another man, and is this how she makes up for his absence, when he, Manish, isn't around? Does Rupa not find him desirable anymore? Maybe she has never loved him, never wanted him. Manish shakes his head in agony and, all of a sudden, he is in a rage. Women are two-faced creatures. They lift up their faces in the pretense of love but bring their grudges to bed. You never know who you are sleeping with.

Manish closes his eyes and a multitude of women seem to leap up at him, jeering. He grinds his teeth. Women are at the root of all problems. They are untrustworthy creatures. Even the scriptures and holy books say so. The laws of Manu, the truisms of old patriarchs, they are relevant even today, and with good reason! Look at Rupa! A hiss escapes through his gritted teeth. Manish stares into space, misery stinging his eyes. Then another thought distracts him: Is she tempting me? But she didn't know I'd be returning home so early.

He turns to look at the bedroom door. There's an embroidered Ganesha, one of Rupa's earlier pieces, hanging on the wall near the door. A gecko peeps out from behind the Ganesha and chuck-chucks apologetically. But the afternoon refuses to give up its gruff silence. Manish's back is stiff, his throat parched. Restaurant food always makes him thirsty. He gingerly eases himself out of the chair. He picks up one of the bottles from the table and drinks until it is almost empty. From across the hall he hears the low conch-honk of a fart and the sound of the toilet flushing. She has not bothered to shut the bathroom door, which she usually does. Immersed in his thoughts, Manish forgets caution and clears his throat.

Rupa rushes out, a strangled scream escaping her lips. She sees him and appears relieved, but just as quickly her expression changes into one of bewilderment. Manish cannot help noticing that she looks neither guilty nor embarrassed.

Almost as a reflex, she asks, 'How come you're home so early?' And, then, she is immediately concerned. 'Are you feeling all right?'

'Yes. Yes,' he says. 'Of course I'm all right. Just the lunch. All that rich stuff doesn't agree with me anymore.' He pauses, but continues to look at her steadily. 'You know that, don't you?' he adds testily.

'I'll make you some ginger tea.' Rupa goes into the kitchen. He catches the scent of soap. He is sure he can smell something else on her as well, but cannot be certain. She is also wearing her caftan inside out.

'You're wearing it wrong,' he says. When she looks at him quizzically, he points out her caftan.

'I came out in a hurry. You startled me.'

'Who did you think had gotten into the house?'

'I don't know. A burglar maybe… But this is such a secure locality.' She searches his face. 'When did you come?'

'Just now,' says Manish, not looking at her. His head has begun to reel again.

'You're not looking well at all,' she says, fussing over him. She puts out a hand to feel his forehead.

Manish waves her away. 'Why don't you wear that thing properly? Go change. I don't want tea. Just some antacid will do.'

Rupa hurries off to change her clothes. She hasn't noticed the spoon, but Manish can't care less now. The moment has passed. Now that she believes he is unwell, he can almost feel a burning sensation in his stomach. But she will see the spoon sooner or later. He will have to explain. He is not even sure if she will appreciate it. He is uncertain all of a sudden.

'Can any man ever know a woman?' he asks himself.

Rupa comes out after a while wearing a printed voile sari in a soft fuchsia shade with a narrow turquoise border. The colour of her blouse matches the sari border. She has pinned up her hair, and even stuck a small turquoise bindi on her forehead.

'I made kachoris today,' she says, bustling around the kitchen. 'Do you remember how many you ate that day when you came to our house for the first time? And how everybody laughed? But I won't give you any now.'

She turns towards him, not quite smiling, but there is a slight tenderness on her face. 'Not today,' she says. 'Plain ginger tea for you now, and a light khichri for dinner afterwards.'

Manish stares at her. He sits down again. What a fool he has been. She has not changed at all. Nothing has. What time was it when he pocketed the spoon? Two? Two-thirty? And what had prompted him to do so? She must have been thinking of their early days too. Probably for longer than he had. Why else would she make kachoris today of all days? She has stopped giving him deep-fried snacks a long time ago. Health was her primary concern these days, and she was always watching cookery programmes and reading up magazines for tips and recipes.

There has to be a connection here, he tells himself. A telepathic one. Maybe that was why he had stolen the spoon. Yes. That must be why. She was thinking of him.

'Look,' he says, almost jumping up, holding the spoon aloft. 'See what I brought!'

The glow from the kitchen's neon tube makes it gleam like silver. He advances towards her, looming larger and larger as he nears. Rupa turns, and her eyes catch some of the tube's white light as they travel upwards. Something rises on her face, and subsides again. The change is so fleeting that Manish isn't sure it happened. And the sigh expelled through barely parted lips could have been just the ceiling fan slicing air in the living room.

Rupa dutifully reaches for the spoon. Manish responds immediately, almost reflexively, raising his hand higher, forcing her to stand on her toes. Subconsciously he marvels at how his body remembers the game they used to play every time he brought one home, soon after they were married.

She has extended an arm now, full length, towards him, while the other lags behind like a reluctant partner in crime. He sees her raised hand, its palm spread open, hanging in the thin as sheet air between them. And just as suddenly, like all the impulses, actions and thoughts that have taken hold of this unusual day, he sees not her hand, but something else: a small bird suspended motionless between them, about to drop dead in mid-flight.

Black Prince

Biren eases his lean body out of bed with the soundless agility born of long practice. He glances at the woman snoring in the far corner of the Burma teak four-poster. She does not stir. He knows she won't. No movement can awaken Supriya. He wouldn't be surprised if she slept through an earthquake. He slips out of the still room. Stale air falls back before the morning breeze that rushes in as he opens the doors.

Biren sucks in fresh air through his barely parted lips, relishing it the way he would a cup of Darjeeling tea. Even so, a spider-silk skein of sorrow tugs at his heart. Today is the last day. The house also has the forlorn look that comes with packing and dismantling. He is amazed and dismayed as well by the things they have collected. How will Supriya find space for everything in their apartment in Ballygunge Circular Road? Their post-retirement home in Calcutta is spacious, as far as high-rise homes go, but is still no match for this sprawling bungalow.

Biren Dutta's bungalow is one among many in Ishpathnagar which mimics an English borough in its architecture and planning. It sits at one end of a long straight street called Piccadilly Avenue, in the centre of an acre of land bordered by lush lantana and hibiscus hedges that skillfully conceal barbed wire fences. The British, who'd been part owners of the now loss-making steel factory, had been avid gardeners and landscape artists. They loved building towns and neighbourhoods which would remind them of home. So the town is a little replica of the British countryside, complete with manicured gardens and boulevards. A store sells ham and bacon brought down from the piggeries in Ranchi, and an assortment of tinned goods, jams and cheeses, along with more mundane provisions like rice and flour. There is a club with squash and tennis courts, a swimming pool, billiards and card rooms, a dance hall, a library—the works.

In the earlier days of free India, brown sahibs like Biren were allowed to become members of the club, but they had to follow the dress codes and rules of conduct laid down by the British. The Indians, of course, took great pride in upholding them. For instance, you could wear flip-flops to the swimming pool but had to be formally dressed to enter the main building. Ladies were not allowed into the bar, and drank their sherry or gin-and-tonic at the lounge. After the British left, the rules were slightly relaxed. And while the Indian sahibs enjoyed the feeling of not being second-class citizens of their own country, they also rued that they had let some the meticulous rules laid down by their erstwhile masters go somewhat unobserved.

Supriya had fallen in love with this life within months of her marriage to Biren. She had learnt to wear a string of pearls of the correct length around her neck, drape fashionable chiffon saris with just that touch of carelessness that let the shoulder-end almost fall off, and sashay on steel-tipped stilettos. She played canasta with the wives of the other officers in the mornings and whist at the club in the evenings. The tinkle of glasses beneath a tallow-coloured moon and the chink of bone-china tea things before sundown charmed her. As did the tatted doilies on the rattan table in the lawn where she enjoyed her lemonade, and other British niceties such as afternoon jam sessions and Saturday night dances, sherry, the Women's Voluntary Society and fétes. She enjoyed the May Queen Balls too, especially since she had once been crowned May Queen, and had a picture taken of herself receiving the tiara and bouquet from the managing director's wife, a horse-faced British woman who had the disgusting habit, thought Supriya, of delivering the babies of labourers. Rumour had it that she had been a nurse or a midwife in England before she got married and came to India.

In a few years, Supriya blossomed into a full-fledged memsahib, a real lady of leisure. No one would have guessed her origins. The third daughter of a school master in the Tehsil school of Bolpur-Sriniketan, Birbhum district, she had been chosen by Biren's father for her flawless beauty and brought, first to their ancestral mansion in Burdwan, and then, later, to their town house in Grey Street, Calcutta, where she had been taught English by an Anglo-Indian lady before being allowed to join Biren. Supriya was clever and eager; she learned her lessons well. She was more or less conversant in English when she came to Biren's bungalow and, once there, quickly learned to command the cook and bearers, the gardeners and sweepers. She spent the afternoons practising English and learning dance steps and English etiquette under the eagle eyes of another Anglo-Indian teacher. In the evenings she shared notes with new brides like herself.

A good and dutiful son, Biren had done exactly what had been expected of him. He had studied metallurgy in Germany, joined the firm where his father's snooker friend from Calcutta Club was a general manager, and had then married Supriya without ever having laid eyes upon her. Perhaps his father knew that left to himself Biren would sooner join art classes at Santiniketan's Viswa Bharati University. Which, incidentally, was the place Supriya began to associate herself with instead of the humbler Sriniketan-Bolpur, turning her school-master father into a professor with a casual wave of manicured hands. Perhaps Biren also knew he would never amount to much anyway, and this town where social life took precedence over productivity was the best option for him. As it was with everything his father decided for him, Biren reckoned, his marriage too was for the best. He did not consider himself rebellious. He was happy to be the way he was, being led through life like many other men with inherited wealth.

Supriya's physical attractions were considerable. She was also a gracious hostess, a natural. Yet a deep dislike towards her seeped into his veins soon after their marriage. However, he kept his dislike in check, more from fear of the gossip it would generate than out of love and respect or a sense of duty towards his family.

Biren stood by and looked on as Supriya took charge of everything in his life. At times, nearly paralysed with disgust, he watched her plot and scheme over the pettiest of things, raging and fuming whenever she didn't get her way. She also took Biren's career into her hands. He didn't protest when she began socializing with his British bosses, who lived away from their wives and families for nearly four months a year, every year, at the beginning of summer. Biren watched as she tottered in late at night on a Wednesday or a Friday, her sari almost slipping off, one hook on her low-cut sleeveless blouse undone.

The card parties were held on those two days, and they both knew that when those parties ended, others would begin. Biren got his promotions, and accepted them quietly, even meekly. He gave Supriya the rewards she demanded every time: jewellery handcrafted by the best johuris of Calcutta.

In time, Biren dutifully sired children; two boys who went to the local school run by the Jesuits until they were ten and were then packed off to a boarding school in the hills. Supriya's morning canasta sessions continued, and so did her other engagements in the club but, over the years, the late-night parties became ordinary get-togethers. They generated less gossip and were mostly frequented by brown officers like themselves as the British and other Europeans quietly abandoned the sinking steel factory and went back home. And, in time, Biren's dislike of his wife became an abiding hatred which festered like a cluster of pus-filled boils, and which he kept hidden—or believed he did. It was then that the first signs of a peptic ulcer appeared. But he did not reduce the sundowners or avoid rich food.

A doctor advised Biren to take up gardening to ease the ulcer in his stomach. Biren took the advice seriously.

Biren's gardener was only too happy to serve a master who took an active interest in his work. And the garden soon flourished with an abundance of blossoms on carefully nurtured plants. Their ambitions for the garden grew as well, and soon the first of the roses were planted. The gardener wisely began with the hardier, more adaptable roses, like the hybrid tea rose and floribunda varieties. When these flowered successfully, he planted some old English roses whose cream-coloured blooms hung in scented bunches above a bamboo arch in a corner of the lawn. Biren inspected his rose garden every day. He excitedly discussed the possibility of growing a Black Prince, not the easiest of roses to grow. The gardener obediently procured a sapling, but it wilted after a week. Biren was disappointed but did not give up. He gave the gardener money and sent him to a well-known nursery a couple of towns away. The second attempt yielded little more than foliage. But at least the plant had survived, Biren consoled himself with this thought. By the time the third set of saplings arrived, Biren was no longer content to merely issue orders. He wanted to, indeed needed to, sink his fingers into the soil, stir the cowdung-and-fermented oil-cake slurry, cut away the browning leaves and infected canes when the dreaded black spot or mildew struck.

Biren's days began with roses and ended with them. Supriya didn't complain. Growing roses was a genteel hobby; besides, they added a certain class to their garden which had quickly become the talk of the town and the envy of her friends. She wanted Biren to enter his roses for the annual flower competitions, but he refused. Much to her surprise, for the first time, she could not bully him into submission. She did not realize that Biren's love for his flowers went much further than the merely proprietorial. Just as she did not know that he had a name for each bush, shrub and creeper, and that he spoke to them softly, caressed their thorny stems, and gently prodded the core of each flower with a lover's finger. Sometimes he would even put his mouth upon petals and tongue them ever so delicately.

The fame of Biren's roses spread far and wide. Strangers often arrived to exchange notes or simply admire them. Biren welcomed these strangers home more warmly than he did his colleagues. Somebody called the roses 'Biren's Beauties' and the name stuck after the usual round of jokes and innuendoes in-between sips of whisky-sour. Biren refused to leave the bungalow even when he became eligible for bigger and better quarters. Supriya fumed, but once again, for the second time in their marriage, she hit a dead end with Biren. In the end she accepted defeat but contented herself by getting the town administrator to sanction a couple of extra rooms and another bathroom.

It took Supriya months to win over the man's betel nut-chewing wife, and endless trips to their house with dishes prepared by her cook. Supriya sacrificed many canasta sessions but she persisted, and won. Afterwards, it was Biren's turn to be put upon, and for many months he and his roses endured the tramping of workmen, the noise and the dust. Some of the roses suffered irreparable damage. Biren took to covering the bushes closest to the house with plastic sheets. He became irritable and developed a cough. His doctor prescribed tonics, but Biren refused to drink them. Instead, he consulted the gardeners at the local horticultural garden and nurseries for concoctions for his precious roses.

By the middle of the year their bungalow had two extra bedrooms with attached baths and a study. The bricks and cement, whitewash and paint were cleared away. Supriya set about decorating the rooms, and Biren's roses were able to breathe again. They flourished and bloomed once more, and when Supriya was finally ready to throw a housewarming party for her new rooms, the roses did her proud by filling the late autumn night with their rich scents, undaunted by the kebabs being cooked over a charcoal fire in the kitchen garden.

Biren added new roses every season. He mourned when a plant died, rejoiced like a new father when a new addition arrived or a new shoot sprang up. By the time his retirement date loomed large, more than fifty varieties of roses and nearly a hundred plants flourished. The roses had slowly taken over more than half the garden, leaving only a patch of lawn in front and a small vegetable garden near the kitchen.

Supriya had watched and said nothing. But as his days

diminished, and retirement became a reality, she rejoiced at the thought of Biren in their Calcutta apartment. How many roses can you grow in a flat, after all? She had never forgiven him for not allowing her to hold their elder son's wedding reception in their own house; it had been her third defeat at Biren's hands, and had rubbed her raw. Relatives and house guests had to be housed in another bungalow that had luckily been lying vacant at that time. Even the festivities had to be hosted there, while her house bore a deserted look, except for the roses.

She had attacked him viciously a few months before their son's marriage but, instead of buckling down, he had fought back. For the first time in her entire married life, she had been shocked and frightened. Biren had flared up, his anger a pure physical thing as he rounded on her. Even his facial features seemed to shift and become something else, and she suddenly wasn't sure if she knew him at all. Afterwards she had meekly gone about preparing the other bungalow for the wedding.

It hadn't turned out to be all that inconvenient, being only a few houses away, though she wouldn't admit it. In fact, Supriya was often glad to be able to return to a quiet house away from the bustle of the wedding. But her ego had been bruised. And, to make matters worse, Biren did not even pretend to make amends. She bitterly acknowledged to herself that she could never come between him and his roses, let alone harm them. Biren's

retirement was her only chance at revenge. She thought
of him roaming around their apartment in his pyjamas,
a dazed look on his face and a catalogue for roses under
his arm. It brought her peace when she lay her head
down on her pillow late in the night.

~

The air is grey and chilly though winter is still a month
away. Biren opens the double doors that lead out to the
veranda circling the front of the house and steps out.
Goose pimples erupt on his arms and chest. He hugs
himself as he steps out. Dead insects lie in small heaps
beneath the lamps that had been lit along the driveway
in the evening. Cold pearls of dew wobble on the grass,
the leaves and the railings. The birds have long been
awake and Biren listens to their full-throated songs with
pleasure. Diwali is already over, yet the air still carries a
certain aura of festivity about it. On any other occasion,
he would have felt completely happy, but today a dead
weight sits upon his heart. He wants to go up to each
rosebush, creeper and rambler, and weep.

Unmindful of the damp, and the sudden sharp things
embedded in the ground below his bare feet, Biren walks
with purposeful steps towards the plant closest to him.
It's a gladiator rose, one that he has propped up against
a pillar of the veranda. The brilliant pink blossoms
surround him with their light fragrance. It is like being

embraced by a lover. One of the low-hanging roses holds dew and, when he touches it, the chill from the little droplets shoots up his arm. He meets each plant and greets it. He goes up to each bush, climber and shrub. The garden is quiet except for the breeze that whispers through the leaves; the birds have stopped singing, but they are there, watching their friend. The roses fling their myriad scents at him, each a special olfactory emissary.

Biren comes to the Black Prince finally. The plant has grown old and its stems are quite woody. But it still produces blossoms of the same velvety dark red which give off a sharp but not overpowering scent. He feels his heart rip at the sight of his Black Prince. And, without warning, the tears begin to flow. He feels the plant from top to bottom, mumbling incoherent words under his breath. He kneels down and, cupping the rose's base with his hands, he closes his eyes. When he opens them again, he sees a shoot of what is unmistakably a tiny young plant, growing about a foot away from the older Black Prince, an uncommon occurrence. The sapling has grown unnoticed and is now big enough to be transplanted to a pot. Biren stares at this parting gift from his beloved rose garden, and feels himself grow tight with emotion.

At this moment, all he wants is to lay himself down upon the soil and give himself to it, this garden, his faithful companion who will remain here while he is forced to uproot himself. He has no idea how long he will be able to survive without it, her. He does not want to think about the inevitable. Now, he just wants is to give himself to her, give until all the fluids in his body have seeped into the soil. He wants to lie there and merge with the earth that holds his roses; to die right there embracing them. The idea ignites in his mind with a lusty flame. He feels his heart beating with more strength.

Biren gets up. He digs with care around the young shoot and gently eases it out. He pats the soil around the roots into a tight ball and carefully places the plant on a table in the veranda before returning to the Black Prince again.

He lies down on the ground beneath his roses, on his back gazing at the sky, now a benign blue above him. When he closes his eyes at last, he sees yellow, not of the sun but of the Judy Garland rose, its flame-coloured petals rimmed with orange. The picture is clear and sharp. The scent of roses descends, heavy and inviting. He turns over and buries his face into the soil.

Salted Pinkies

We were sitting huddled around a table, staring at the peeling walls of Bimal-da's teashop for inspiration, when the man who introduced us to the Grand Canyon pygmy ape walked in.

It was another sodden monsoon evening. We—Partho, Sanjeeb, Suresh, Joy and I—had run out of conversation and cigarettes. We were irritable, and ready to fight, if only to break the monotony of endless days of rain. Partho was even more fidgety, which did nothing to help our mood. At that time we thought it was the rain and boredom, so we put up with his restlessness. Maybe things would have turned out differently had we known what was on his mind. Then again, maybe not.

Partho, with his 32-cup-sized boobs, his jiggling buttocks, and the long nail on his left pinkie which he painted a deep maroon, could easily have passed off for a woman except for the line of fine hair on his upper lip, and the large unfeminine pores on his face. He was effeminate in many ways. Perhaps that's why girls liked him; they considered him their own, and felt safe with him. This was fine by us. The girls came to Partho, he brought them to us. It was a nice arrangement, except that they never became our girlfriends and we kept covering up our virginity with crude jokes. When the rains began, we kept our spirits up by watching drenched women struggle through the often waist-deep water flowing on the road before us. But, after a few days of non-stop downpour, the women began to stay indoors and soon we could see only men, cursing as they waded through the water, struggling to balance their umbrellas and their slippers, which they held close to their bosoms like prize-winning lottery tickets.

We sat with the dregs of our tea in Bimal-da's teashop—a gloomy room and a sooty airless kitchen at the back. He sold tea, coffee, aerated drinks and oily snacks. He employed two boys, Makhon and Sambhu, to serve the customers and to cook and clean. We were low on cash, so tea was all we could afford. Bimal-da didn't mind. Business was down anyway, and we were old customers. Besides, Bimal-da enjoyed having us around. Like many old-timers of Calcutta, he liked the idea of hosting conversations on politics and poetry in his teashop. Perhaps he thought he was creating a haven for the erudite future leaders of the nation, after the famous College Street Coffee House. Sometimes Bimal-da and his boys would join us when we argued about cricket. Sometimes the other customers would join in, too. Bimal-da didn't sell too many snacks or cups of tea when that happened, but he was happy.

Mind you, this was in the early eighties, when we called our city Calcutta (or Cal for short) in English and Kolkata in Bengali, and the transition from one to the other posed no questions of disloyalty to the mother tongue. You could openly call yourself a Marxist; in fact, you had better call yourself one, or at least appear to have Leftist leanings. Jobs were scarce, and young men like us thronged teashops like Bimal-da's. If you had a job, all the aunts and grandmothers of the locality would try their hand at finding a good girl for you. If you were brilliant and lucky, you became one of those fabled folks who lived abroad. And anything foreign or 'foreign–returned' made everyone delirious.

No wonder we were eaten up by curiosity when the man, who looked like a foreign-returned fellow, entered the teashop. He wore smart clothes and had a rugged physique, but his face was fleshy and unattractive. We sniffed his perfume.

'Brut?' whispered Suresh.

Sanjeeb gave him a withering look. 'Brut? Nobody who is anybody uses Brut!'

Sanjeeb had an elder brother who worked somewhere in the US. I don't think the brother was as prosperous as Sanjeeb made him out to be, but we still accepted his superior knowledge about all things that came from the western hemisphere, things that we could only read about in the rare foreign magazines that came our way. The man looked like he needed to be somewhere dry until the weather cleared up. We were certain he wouldn't mind shelling out the one rupee for a cup of hot sweet tea in exchange for temporary shelter. Many of Bimal-da's customers were like that. Sometimes a guy might come in with his girlfriend and instantly brighten up the surroundings. We looked forward to those occasions. Bimal-da did, too, because when a couple walked in, the boyfriend would almost certainly buy snacks along with the tea, coffee or soda. Sometimes, on a rainy day like this one, there might be well-dressed blokes who dropped in, either alone or in small groups, looking like gilt-collared Chihuahuas in a garbage dump full of mongrels. Those rare shelter-seekers would keep to themselves and take quick sips from their cola bottles. Our stranger, however, did nothing of that sort. He did not hug a corner, looking uncomfortable because his present surroundings were below his status. Instead, he walked in briskly, giving the room a quick sweeping glance which included Partho for a second or so. Partho squirmed in his seat and took to chewing his thumb. The man turned towards Bimal-da who was sitting at his cash desk, waiting expectantly.

'Terrible evening to be out,' he said in the accented

Bengali spoken by those Bengalis who have been living abroad for long. Some of them are fakes; the accents I mean. There are those who put on an accent because they think that speaking Bengali the way we do shows a lack of class. We can tell a fake Bengali accent from a real one. But this guy's accent was genuine.

'Yes, terrible weather,' replied Bimal-da affably.

'I could use some tea and snacks,' said the stranger, and immediately endeared himself to Bimal-da.

'What would you like?'

'Oh. I don't really know,' he said, sounding bashful. 'What would you recommend?'

Bimalda's eyes gleamed behind his spectacles. 'Makhon,' he called. 'What's hot in the kitchen? Quickly!'

Makhon came out of the hole right up to Bimal-da, wiping his hands on an oily cloth and grinning from ear to ear. 'Mutton samosas!'

Bimalda frowned. Mutton samosa was the most expensive item on his menu, and didn't sell as much as his vegetable samosas and egg pakoras. So, in all likelihood, the mutton samosas were stale. Bimalda didn't want to create a bad impression in front of his new customer. 'Are you sure?' he said, hesitantly.

'Arre!' Makhon rolled his eyes. 'Why would I lie? You gave me money to buy the mutton keema this morning only. I spent the whole afternoon preparing the filling and rolling the dough and…'

'Okay, okay,' said Bimalda and turned to his customer. 'You will have mutton samosas with tea or coffee?'

The man smiled. 'Hot tea, please.'

Makhon hurried back to the kitchen and Sambhu slid out almost immediately after him. He wiped a table-top, smiled, and backed away. The man nodded and sat down. Makhon came in with the samosas and laid them down with a flourish. Sambhu, not to be outdone, hurried up with a cup of steaming hot tea on a slightly chipped saucer that didn't match the cup, and placed on a larger plate that served as tray. Tension steamed up from Bimal-da and misted his spectacles.

The man tried not to smile. He chewed thoughtfully for a minute before exclaiming, 'This is very good!' He then turned abruptly towards us: 'It's such a pity that I should be the only one to eat such nice and hot mutton samosas. Why don't you gentlemen join me?'

We stared at him. The man was friendly and he had money to throw. But why would a complete stranger want to buy us mutton samosas and tea? Suresh, Joy and Sanjeeb shifted in their chairs. But Partho, smiling like a moron, was already standing up. I tugged at his sleeve. 'Show some self-respect, you greedy pig!' I hissed. Partho wobbled and flopped back into his chair.

'Sorry,' said the man standing up. 'I should have introduced myself. I'm Anoop Batobyal. I'm here for a short visit,' he said, walking towards us.

Anoop shook hands with all of us, including Bimal-da, and smiled disarmingly. Things seemed to move smoothly after that. His easy affability and lack of airs made us relax. Besides, who wanted to forgo a free treat? We were soon engrossed in small talk. Even Bimal-da left his post by the cash desk and joined us. He wasn't expecting any more customers. Besides, this one customer had brought rich pickings. Makhon and Sambhu came over after a while, and listened open-mouthed, resting their glistening hands on the backs of the grease-darkened chairs.

After the usual introductory small talk, conversation drifted to foreign countries, cultures and cuisines. Sanjeeb took the lead for a while, as he was the only one qualified to match—or rather, pretend to match—the stranger's superior knowledge. Suresh and I contributed a bit, putting in a word here, asking a suitable question there. Joy remained quiet. After some time, the man leaned back in his chair and sighed.

'Is anything troubling you?' lisped Partho.

He shook his head, looked at us with a slight smile, and said, 'All this talk about other places and other foods and dietary habits reminds me...' He paused, as if seeking permission to proceed.

'Oh, do tell us,' lisped Partho again.

'Yes, yes,' said Bimal-da. 'Nothing like a good story over hot tea on a rainy day!'

'You know this earth is such a strange place. It's full of surprises,' said Anoop Batobyal… 'Just when you've decided you've seen everything there is to see on this planet, gone everywhere and done everything, you discover a new place, a new people and a new culture. Amazing, isn't it?' Everybody nodded. 'But the most amazing thing about people is the food that they eat. I mean, take the aborigines of Australia, they eat the witchetty grub. You know, it's a kind of worm!'

'Ugh!' said Bimal-da.

Makhon and Sambhu snickered. Sanjeeb gravely nodded.

'Koreans eat dogs,' said Joy, breaking his silence.

'Yes,' said Anoop. 'There is nothing wrong with these food habits. But of course, one man's meat is another's poison.' He sighed softly.

'We ate pig's trotters at Tangra once.' Partho giggled, looking at us. 'Remember?'

'Ai Ma!' said Sambhu.

'Keep quiet, Sambhu,' said Bimal-da.

The man licked the tips of his fingers delicately. 'Are there any mutton samosas left?'

Makhon looked sheepish. Bimal-da looked embarrassed. 'Actually, I don't make too many of those, you see,' he explained. 'Not many people can afford… I like to serve only fresh food, you know.' Bimal-da nodded at all of us. We nodded in agreement. 'How about some more tea?' he asked hopefully.

'Sure. Very welcome in fact. And with the tea, I will provide some snacks of my own.' Anoop smiled genially at Bimal-da, adding, 'With your permission, of course.' He produced a couple of foil packets from a bag I hadn't noticed before. The packets looked foreign-made, but were unfamiliar. And the words on the packets were written in an unknown language.

'What are these?' asked Partho. He had already dipped his fat fingers into one that Anoop had obligingly opened for him.

'They look like French fries,' said Sanjeeb.

'Salted pinkies,' said Anoop casually.

'What kind of a name is "Salted Pinkies?"' I asked.

'Exactly!' said Sanjeeb. 'My brother never mentioned it!'

'They are called "salted pinkies" because that's exactly what they are,' saidAnoop, glancing fleetingly at Partho, who was munching away contentedly. The rest of us stopped chewing.

'What do you mean?' I asked.

'They are the roasted little pinkies of the Grand Canyon pygmy ape.'

Bimal-da's jaw fell open. Makhon and Sambhu squealed. Suresh hastily dropped the handful he'd fished out back into the packet. Joy, without bothering about good manners, quickly spat out his mouthful into a saucer. Sanjeeb frowned.

'These animals are found nowhere else on earth,' continued Anoop. 'They are so small that even a six-year-old child is a good head taller than the adult male Grand Canyon pygmy ape. They have pale skins covered with soft, tawny, sometimes golden fur; the colour helps them disappear into the vast canyons. For their predators are many. The puma and man, to name just two. You see, these apes have extraordinarily sweet and tender flesh. They have been eaten by the indigenous people living in the canyons for centuries. Every part of their body is a delicacy. Top restaurants in New York, Milan, Paris, London and Tokyo serve their meat baked, roasted, stir-fried or pan-seared. But never ever curried. You see, their meat is so tender that it would melt away in a curry, bone and all. High-end restaurants charge huge prices for a single serving. It's never announced in their menu cards. You have to know the chef personally. So it's not merely the very rich who can taste the flesh of the Grand Canyon pygmy ape. You have to be both very rich and very influential.'

We stared dumbfounded.

'But now their numbers have dwindled substantially. Even though much of the world does not know of the existence of these creatures, gourmets have almost wiped them out. Now the US government is very worried about the future of this species. If the last ape falls, the super-rich of the world will lose the taste and texture of extraordinarily delicious meat. We must save the apes. If only for our taste-buds.'

Partho leaned forward, rapt. Anoop looked at him and smiled absently. I watched the effect of his speech on Partho. Sanjeeb almost snarled. I quickly kicked him underneath the table in warning. Suresh and Joy maintained serious faces, but their twitching lips were getting harder to ignore. Bimal-da and his boys continued to stare, their mouths open.

'What are you going to do?' whispered Partho.

I looked at Partho in disgust. Suresh must have felt the same way. He asked me for a cigarette, even though he rarely smoked. I didn't have any left. Nor did anyone else. Anoop was obviously a non-smoker; he had that look about him. 'Suck on one of these,' I suggested. But Suresh shook his head. I took a pinkie and put it between my lips, letting it dangle like a cigarette.

Partho passed Anoop some salted pinkies. He smiled, a little sadly it seemed to me, and, accepting a few, scrunched them up and washed them down with what was left of his tea. Partho tittered shyly.

Suresh, Joy and I remained poker-faced, but Sambhu and Makhon were already grinning, while Bimal-da still looked bemused. Sanjeeb's lips had almost curled into a grimace. Joy stretched his legs and yawned. I looked at my watch. It was almost a quarter to ten. High time we went home. The others must have felt the same way. I saw Bimal-da make a swift sign at his boys. They went back to the kitchen to prepare dinner before closing for the night.

Sanjeeb looked at Anoop with a sarcastic smile on his face. 'So how and where did you manage to acquire packets of endangered ape digits?'

Anoop didn't reply, but the look in his eyes made me uncomfortable. I didn't want an ugly scene erupting at this late hour, and that too with someone who had just been buying us tea and snacks. I fidgeted in my chair. 'It's getting late,' I said.

'Oh. I'm so sorry,' he said, genial once again. 'I didn't realize. Different time zones you know… Did I tell you that I landed only a couple of days ago?' I smiled politely. 'Actually,' he continued, 'I am a representative of the Arizona-based company that has the US government's permission to farm, harvest and sell the ape meat and by-products, as well as to ensure that they don't get wiped out by poachers. We are also trying to create a hybrid species with our apes and the Indian rhesus macaques to get a breed that will retain the exquisite flesh of the original beasts, but be more resilient. There is an acute shortage of Grand Canyon pygmy apes, so many fakes are being sold to restaurants. The chefs are naturally worried about their reputations… So you could say I am a sort of emissary of the US government sent to India to garner cooperation in this top-secret project.'

'Top-secret project, eh?' said Sanjeeb, his voice dripping with sarcasm. 'So, how come you just shared your top secret with us? Won't you get into trouble with your US government?'

I thought, 'Oh, oh, now there'll be a scene.' But nothing happened. Anoop ignored Sanjeeb's jibe and laughed almost apologetically. 'We are looking for passionate people to help us in the cause… But let me not keep you gentlemen,' he said in a friendly way.

Bimal-da, who had no further interest in the customer after being paid in crisp rupee notes, drifted off to his desk and busied himself with the accounts. Suresh and Joy smartly shook Anoop's hand, thanked him for the treat and mumbled 'hope to meet you again' before sauntering out. They had obviously had enough. That left Sanjeeb, Partho and me. I hesitated. I was a little ashamed about the way my friends were treating him. But who did Anoop Batobyal from United States think we were? A bunch of oafs and bumpkins? Just because we didn't have money and hadn't travelled across the world? We were jobless, not brainless! He had no business to make fools out of us. Did he really think that we'd believe him? I didn't want to confront him though. But Sanjeeb had an ego, and I could see that he wasn't about to let Anoop go so easily. He watched Anoop with narrowed eyes, his hands in his pockets. 'You are looking for recruits?'

'Yes,' said Anoop, looking serious. 'And I think I have already found one.'

Partho blushed. 'I know I'm being impulsive. But you must understand that it's very important to save those creatures.'

'What!' Sanjeeb and I said together.

'Are you out of your mind?' I raised my hand in a mock slap. Partho winced.

'Saala gandu!' shouted Sanjeeb. I was afraid he would beat Partho, who looked ready to weep. Then I noticed that he had stuck out his lower lip. Partho was going to be stubborn.

The sudden hullaballoo brought Makhon, Sambhu, Joy, Suresh and Bimal-da running back. 'Partho has just made up his mind to save the pygmy apes,' I said, jerking a thumb at the two of them. Everybody burst out laughing, except for the duo. After a minute, they walked out without a word. We could only stare. We had never seen Partho behave like this.

Sanjeeb was the first to recover. 'Hey! Hey Partho! Saala! You mad or what? Come back right now!'

The rest of us ran out, shouting, 'Partho! Partho!'

They were nowhere to be seen.

Suresh wondered aloud about Anoop Batobyal and his strange story. Joy and I laughed quietly. We all agreed that listening to that fellow was a small price to pay for hot samosas and tea on a boring evening. But Partho's behaviour worried us. None of us could believe that he had actually walked out. So, after searching for him somewhat half-heartedly, we gave up and hung around, talking. We were there for longer than we realized and wondered if we should go looking for Partho again. Seriously, this time. Bimal-da had already shut shop and gone home. His boys were warmly ensconced inside, probably fast asleep.

We started to walk up and down the streets randomly, looking into the lanes and bylanes that crisscrossed each other. 'Partho! Partho!' we shouted. But there was no answer.

'If that gandu doesn't turn up by tomorrow, we'll have to make a police report,' said Suresh.

'Who'll believe this cock and bull story?' said Joy. 'What shit! And, we let the bugger talk just because he bought samosas for us?'

'Hey. That time we weren't taking him seriously. Who knew Partho would fall for his crap…?' I didn't get to finish.

Sanjeeb gripped my shoulder. 'Saala! Of course! How did I miss it?'

'What?' we all cried, stopping in our tracks.

'Fall! Didn't you just say fall? That's it. That's what happened. Partho's fallen for this guy. Don't you see? His impulsiveness is just an act. He planned it!'

'No! That's bullshit. He met the fellow only today!' said Joy. 'Right?'

'Besides,' said Suresh, 'our Partho isn't a bloody homo,

yaar. Why would he do something as…as indecent as that? Seriously, Partho's not a homo…'

At that time none of us truly believed that Partho preferred men over women, though I guess in our heart of hearts we knew. Partho had never hit on any of us. We were his buddies. All of us had grown up together in the same street. Partho often got the butt end of our jokes. Like the time—we were just thirteen or fourteen then—when Sanjeeb had made Partho kneel and pretended to ram him from behind to demonstrate how some women liked it, Partho had first squealed with laughter and then burst into tears. After that we had been gentler with Partho. We protected him from the taunts of school bullies and funny men on the streets. We accepted his femininity; there were other boys like him, we knew. They all outgrew their feminine streak after marriage. In time, so would Partho. That was all there was to it. As for the man, he didn't look like a 'homo' to us. Not that any of us knew anyone who did, in actual fact, look like one. In our time such things just didn't happen in traditional and respectable Bengali localities. Sanjeeb was being his usual outrageous self. Joy and Suresh agreed with me when I told them so. But as it turned out, outrageous or not, Sanjeeb was right.

A few weeks later, after the routine of the police report, putting ads in the newspaper etcetera, Partho's heartbroken mother received a letter from him, saying that he was well and very 'happily married to the man of his dreams', and also that 'he was not ashamed of himself'. Lastly, Partho said that he had been compelled to take this extreme step because we were 'cruel and insensitive'. He would be migrating, but he didn't mention where to or when. He asked for his poetry books, a few paintings that he had done and some favourite articles of clothing to be packed. He would send someone to collect them, but his family was not to be rude to his 'emissary'. He asked for his mother's blessings and hoped we would understand. He wanted us, his friends, to know how much he loved us and that he hadn't meant to hurt our feelings. He did not mention when, where and how he had met his 'husband'. Nobody knew which country the happy couple was migrating to, or where they were living at the moment.

We winced throughout the reading of the letter. Partho's father was outraged. 'How dare he!' he said. 'What does he mean by saying he's gay? He has blackened my face! Henceforth I have no son. Let everyone know that my only son is dead.'

The elderly people who had gathered nodded their heads in agreement and looked disapprovingly at us. Partho's mother beat her breasts and wept inconsolably. 'Partho is a very good boy. A good boy who has been led astray,' she wailed, and looked at us accusingly.

Partho's four unmarried older sisters looked

embarrassed and confused. His father, after pronouncing he had no son, now openly blamed us for not keeping an eye on Partho. The police dispersed making lewd remarks. The neighbours smirked. We came away from that house of grief, unable to either defend ourselves or explain Partho's behaviour.

We felt betrayed. Partho should have told us, he could have trusted us a little. We were puzzled, too. Partho had obviously met the fellow some time ago; how had he managed to keep his relationship under wraps? We felt very naïve and unsophisticated. The whole locality was abuzz with the news of Partho's elopement. Some claimed that he had always acted suspiciously, but they had all been too innocent to realize it. Otherwise, they said, he would have received the beating of his life and been cured of his homosexuality. And everyone speculated about how he had managed to start and carry on an affair, and with a probashi Bengali in the first place. There were as many theories as there were jokes.

We continued to gather at Bimal-da's. We had nowhere else to go. We told Sambhu to serve us tea. We smoked our cigarettes. We sat in morose silence. Then, one day, Joy burst out laughing.

'What assholes we are! Saala! He got us by our balls! We never even got a whiff of what he was up to. Right under our very noses, too! What a chhupa Rustom! Wonder who that fellow was and where Partho found him?'

Joy's words released something within us. We laughed, too. Partho had outsmarted us. He had also liberated himself from the dull routine of an impoverished life. In his own way, he had turned out to be more of a man than any of us. We were the real pariahs, young men without a job or prospects, tolerated by our families and relatives. The moment we acknowledged this, we felt relieved. And, curiously, happy for our Partho.

After some time, Sanjeeb said, 'Okay, so we know the whole thing was a setup by Partho and his, um, boyfriend. But what about the apes? And those things he called salted pinkies? I am guessing they were potato chips past their expiry date. Right?'

We kept quiet, blowing our individual smoke rings and watching them drift away. What did we know? Sanjeeb looked at us for a minute and then went back to studying the smoke rings from his newly lit cigarette. Slumped over his chair, he seemed defeated. Then he straightened up.

'I got a letter from dada,' he said. 'He says he can manage something for me there. Soon. Hopefully.'

The three of us nodded. We understood, but did not utter the words that sat like stones in our throats, corking up the agitation within.

Ahalya

halya runs like a carefree deer towards the top of the hill. She runs with the wind in her hair, and it undoes the neatness her mother had taken so much care to achieve. Ahalya has all but forgotten her mother's irritation, her harsh words, and the slap. It doesn't take her long to forget things that don't concern her for the moment.

Kanai watches Ahalya as she scampers up. His goats do not need watching. They know these hills better than he does. So he plays his flute, loiters with the other goatherds, or just spends his day idly looking at the passing clouds and dreaming. Dreaming of Ahalya, mostly, and sometimes of their wedding. But this is a dream that only he and his flute know about. Not even the wind knows what's in his heart; such is the secrecy with which he hugs his desire.

Ahalya cannot be bothered by girlish things. She would rather be out playing marbles, climbing trees and fishing with the boys. She is better at being a boy than the boys themselves. She can steal mangoes from right under Kartik Dadu's nose; her nimble fingers can bring down any kite that dares to fly across her square of the sky; she can spin the fastest top and run the longest mile. But most of all—and for this she has the grudging respect of all the boys—she can tolerate the limb-numbingly cold waters of the spring and its astringent clay even during the winter months, the way none of them ever can.

The springs spout from the hill not too far away from the temple of Jagadhartri on the hill's peak. The temple is several hundred years old, and dates back to a time when tantrics were said to have offered human sacrifices to Goddess Kali. Shrines housing lesser deities surround the main temple. These deities are mostly female goddesses of unknown origin who have sprung up from time to time, literally spat out from the black soil roiling in the heart of the hill. Nobody knows when or how these deities originated. They are not wrought by human hand; they are the handiwork of a strange and unknown force. They appeared from time to time in the temple precincts, squeezed out from the cracks on the hill that crisscross its surface. They bear an eerie likeness to the human form, though they are grossly exaggerated in shape and size. However, these black-clay deities have been left mostly exposed to vandals and the vagaries of the weather, and new ones have not appeared in a hundred years.

The clay deities, however, are far from Kanai's mind. He looks on with longing as the wind undoes Ahalya's braids. His heart twitches with love. He and Ahalya have practically grown up together. And though he knows when Ahalya transformed into a woman, having himself reached manhood a few years ago, he cannot remember when he began to feel the way he does for her.

'Kanai, stop staring at me.' Ahalya throws a handful of dry black soil at him. Then, in the same breath, she asks, 'Got guavas?'

Kanai smiles. He finds it hard to do anything else in her presence. 'I brought some coconut naru today. Have those if you like.'

'Thoo! Who wants your naru?' Ahalya runs off, flinging the words at him over her shoulder.

'Wait, Ahalya, wait for me!' cries Kanai. He runs after her. The wind whistles in his ears as he chases her up the hill and stirs the nerves below his navel. His eyes follow Ahalya's lithe movements, and his heart aches.

They stop near the guesthouse built and run by the local municipality. It is used mostly by tourists and visiting officials, and sometimes by pilgrims to the temple. The guesthouse overflows with visitors during peak season, but now stands more or less empty. A few students of art are here to enjoy the off-season rates and paint the surrounding landscape and temple. The locals call the artists sahari babu because that is what they are, city slicks.

Ahalya and other girls of her age are discouraged from mixing with the students. For they are men with beards and long, unkempt hair. And they constantly reek of cigarettes and liquor. They do provide a bit of income for the local boys though. The sahari babus need help with many things. They need their clothes washed and ironed, their food cooked and served, their cigarettes and booze bought and, occasionally, women hired. But though women from the village are brought in ostensibly to be models for the artists, the townsfolk are not convinced about the innocence of these modelling assignments. Ahalya, too, has been strictly forbidden by her mother, Saroma, from hanging around the place. Ahalya, for once, is not defiant. The sahari babus do not interest her. She does not understand why they splash pots of paint indiscriminately on canvas and paper. The tourist lodge, however, has a topa kul tree and its delicious sweet-sour fruits are coveted by all.

The month of Poush is over and the fruits are almost ripe. But Saraswati Puja is still a fortnight away. Ahalya knows eating kul is strictly forbidden before Saraswati Puja. But she does not care. The boys always manage to get and eat them by the handful, and they are the ones who most need Ma Saraswati's blessings if they are to finish school at all. Why should she make this sacrifice? Nobody is going to send *her* to school!

'Kanai, have you seen the topa kul tree?"

Kanai looks at her in alarm. 'Are you thinking of raiding it?'

'What if I am?'

Kanai says nothing. He knows arguing with Ahalya is of no use once she gets an idea into her head. But he is not comfortable being here with her. He does not relish the prospect of any of the sahari babus meeting her. Four or five of them are staying in the guesthouse. They are likely to be inside, drinking their evening tea, and will certainly see Ahalya. Kanai follows Ahalya helplessly through the open gate into the guesthouse garden. He even helps her shake the tree after she has finished inspecting its bounty from below. Ahalya is intent upon her spoils, but Kanai knows they are being watched. The silence underneath the clamour of roosting birds has warned him. But it is already too late.

Kanai is not afraid of what the sahari babus will say or do when they catch him and Ahalya. The locals have as much right to the kul as do the babus. The latter, however, enjoy the servile, simpering support of Haru Buro, the caretaker. Kanai's heart gives a start as he hears the distinctly sibilant sound of air being sucked in through a half-open mouth. He turns around with a sinking feeling.

'Ki re Kanai?' Haru Buro grins at him through paan-stained teeth. 'The kul is ripe for the plucking, eh?'

Haru Buro's tone is not hostile. And this makes Kanai

both afraid and suspicious. Haru Buro is supposed to fly at them with a stick. Instead, he stands there grinning.

'Who is that with you? Is that Ahalya? Arey Ahalya, you've grown so big! You'll remember to invite me to your wedding, won't you?'

Ahalya looks at him balefully before spitting a kul seed in his direction. The seed hits Haru's toe with perfect accuracy. 'Who said anything about me getting married!' says Ahalya disdainfully.

Haru Buro chuckles softly to himself. 'So hot-tempered! But don't mind me. Just help yourself. There's plenty for everybody.'

'Of course I will! As if anybody can stop me!' retorts Ahalya.

Kanai uneasily shifts his feet. 'Come Ahalya. You've collected enough today.' Ahalya shrugs. Kanai, beginning to get angry, turns towards Haru Buro. 'How come you're so generous today, eh?' he says. 'You're never one to give things for free, even if they are free! What do you want?'

'There's no need to be so uptight, Kanai,' says Haru. 'Can't an old man like me give something without rousing your suspicions? Besides, I've seen Ahalya since she was a baby. Now, you tell me, why are you following her around? Eh?'

'Haru Buro, you mind your tongue! You think I am a fool!' Kanai turns towards Ahalya who is staring at him, startled by his sudden anger. 'Ahalya, come away. Right now!'

'Arey! Arey! I was just teasing,' says Haru. 'Come, come inside, now. Your kaki has made some lovely topa kul pickle.'

Ahalya's eyes light up. 'Pickle?'

'Ah yes. She was saying she would give some to your mother, but now that you're here, you might as well save your kaki the trouble of going over. You know how her back troubles her. Come now,' says Haru Buro, extending a hand to Ahalya.

'Get the right bait and you'll catch the best fish,' mutters Kanai under his breath as he watches Ahalya skip towards Haru.

Haru Buro must be lying about the pickle. The whole community knows how inept his wife is at any type of kitchen work. The standard joke about them is that Kaki is such a bad cook, everything she cooks turns bitter, but Haru Buro can't tell the difference because his taste buds can only detect bitterness. Besides, even if her pickles turned out to be palatable by some quirk of fate, why would these two bad-tempered people want to give any to Saroma Mashi? Haru Buro is up to something, of that Kanai is certain. But there is little he can do except follow them into the guesthouse kitchen.

The promised jar of pickle is really there on the kitchen counter, as if waiting for Ahalya, but Kaki is nowhere to be seen. Someone else is there though, a stranger who stands quietly in the shadows. And if he has been looking at Ahalya, he is being so discreet that even Kanai doesn't notice. Ahalya looks about her with idle curiosity.

Haru Buro watches her closely.

Ahalya clutches her bundle of topa kul. This is alien territory, and Kanai can tell she's uncertain. The embers from the coal stove in the corner of the kitchen cast a rosy glow upon her face. She is not aware of it, but she looks beautiful. Kanai is, and the sibilant breath tells him that Haru Buro is too.

'Go on, don't be shy,' says Haru. 'Take a look around. Ei Kanai, why don't you go with her? Our Ahalya's feeling shy!'

'Who said anything about being shy?' says Ahalya, stung by Haru's teasing. She marches into the rooms beyond with a toss of her dark hair.

Kanai looks around the kitchen. The man he had barely noticed has melted back into the walls. Haru Buro leers at him and Kanai reluctantly follows Ahalya. Haru Buro follows a little later. The house is suspended in silence. Kanai does not like it at all. He senses something lurking in the air. He is not really surprised when Ahalya gives a little scream. But his heart thuds wildly all the same.

'O Ma! Look at this!' Ahalya stands in wonder before a black-and-white sketch propped up on a table.

A large oil lamp throws its amber light on the

drawing. A neon tubelight's pale illumination washes across the room. The oil lamp isn't necessary, and Kanai realizes with a shock that the lamp has been placed there on purpose: to draw attention to the sketch. Kanai stares at the picture and a ball of ice grows in his heart.

It is Ahalya, caught in a moment of gleeful abandon under the topa kul tree. The sketch is hasty, but it has perfectly captured Ahalya's posture. Her strands of untidy hair, her delighted eyes, and her young, lithe body. Kanai looks on as Ahalya lifts the drawing with rare reverence. He can sense that she is already slipping away into another world.

Haru Buro asks, 'Who is that girl in the picture, Ahalya?'

Ahalya shakes her head.

'Why it's you, you crazy girl!' Haru gives Ahalya a friendly push. Ahalya is too caught up with the drawing to notice his impertinence.

'Who drew it?' she finally asks.

'One of the artists staying here,' says Haru Buro. 'I'm not sure which one. You want to see some of their paintings?'

Haru propels Ahalya towards a door the moment she nods her head. Kanai trails after them, unsure about what to do. They examine a dozen paintings stacked around the room in various stages of completion. The paintings are good. They are not abstract art, but realistic figures of men and women. Kanai recognizes Haru Buro's wife in one of them, cutting fish on a rusty bonthi by the tap in the courtyard.

'They can make paintings like this of you,' hisses Haru Buro. Ahalya listens with her head to one side. Kanai watches closely. 'Like they make paintings of queens and princesses!'

Ahalya turns towards Haru with mesmerized eyes. A tiny smile of wonder turns up the corners of her lips. 'Really? Haru Kaka, they can do drawings of me like that?' And, then she turns to admire the paintings once more. Kanai watches, and despair chills his heart.

~

'You're wicked and stupid! You are not going there back again. As for this pickle,' Saroma screams, picking up the jar, 'I won't have it in my house!' She hurls it out the door.

Ahalya says nothing. But her face has a dreamy look. In the distance, a little beyond the verandah, the pickle jar shatters and spills its contents on to the cobbled lane. The tiny house sinks back into an uneasy silence. Saroma sniffles into a corner of her sari. Ahalya is quiet. She does not seem to be aware of anything amiss. Kanai, standing outside in the shadows, hears it all, the words and the silences. A dim moon strokes the tears on his cheeks, and they glisten like the shards on the cobbles.

Saroma does not confine Ahalya to the house. It

is enough for them to keep a close watch on Ahalya's movements, she tells Kanai. Saroma does not want any talk. If the women of their neighbourhood come to know, their gossip will kill any chance of marriage for Ahalya.

Kanai is glad to be included in Saroma's plans. But he cannot say the one thing that could get him his heart's desire. The words are in his throat. But every time Saroma talks to him about Ahalya, Kanai can feel the words clotting up deep inside his chest, too far down for him to spit out. Kanai is ashamed to tell her about the ways Ahalya has changed. He is puzzled, too. Overnight, she seems to have blossomed into a woman; not just any woman, but one who knows the secret powers of her body. Their Ahalya has grown sly as well, and crafty. She finds new ways to escape without being detected every day. She has acquired the determined skills of the desperately obsessed. And Kanai, like a rodent hypnotized by a snake, finds it impossible to escape her net of deception. Willy-nilly, he becomes Ahalya's accomplice, instead of the custodian he had promised Saroma he would be.

Kanai does not know if the babus are really painting her portrait or not. Ahalya has only shown him a few charcoal sketches on scraps of rough drawing paper. Haru Buro whispers sibilantly that Ahalya will be famous; she will bring pride and prosperity to their town. Old Haru is full of whispers and ideas these days.

'You know Kanai, this is art. Art!' he says. 'There is nothing sinful about art. And Ahalya is a natural model.' Haru Buro rubs his hands together, as if he is expecting a windfall himself.

'I want to be there when they are painting her,' says Kanai, finally, in desperation.

Haru's pale brown eyes glint in the afternoon sun. 'All right,' he says slowly, 'I'll ask them.'

Kanai has to remind Haru Buro a number of times before he is let inside. When he is finally allowed in, the sahari babus are nowhere to be seen. There is only Ahalya in the room, looking slightly dishevelled. She has a sullen look on her face. Kanai looks at her closely. He feels shy in her presence, as if he had chanced upon her during an intimate moment.

Ahalya looks at him irritably. 'Don't you have anything better to do than spy on me?'

'Ahalya, Saroma Mashi told me …'

'Saroma Mashi told me!' Ahalya cuts in. 'Stupid goat! Herding goats is what you are good for! If your Saroma Mashi tells you to eat dung, you'll eat it?'

Kanai keeps quiet. He feels like an intruder. He does not quite understand why. He looks about the room searching for the easel and canvas. There are several canvasses stacked against the wall.

'Where's the painting?' he says at last. 'You're here because they wanted to paint you…'

Ahalya snorts and gets up to leave. She is wearing silver anklets. They look very pretty on her slender ankles, and make a seductive tinkling sound when she moves. Kanai stares at her feet. Is this the same Ahalya? The girl who used to hate ornaments and pretty things?

'The painting's there, right under your nose,' she says over her shoulder. 'I'm going home now, goatherd!'

Kanai gazes at the painting for a long moment. It *is* Ahalya, but she doesn't look like herself. She is leaning against some kind of a leafy branch that transforms into a snake near her head. She has a satiated smile on her face. She looks older, worldly. Kanai recognizes the look. He shudders as he desperately tries to shut out a thought.

But he cannot escape it. Days pass into weeks, and Kanai still cannot escape it. It sneaks up on him even when he's stretched out on the hill, under the stars. Kanai feels exhausted and saddened. A chilly wind creeps down from the hill and pinches his skin with thin, twiggy fingers. In the distance, he hears a woman laugh. The sound brings back memories of stories he heard when he was a boy, of she-ghosts and witches and black deities that some said were Ma Kali's joginis, sent down by her to keep an eye on the temple and its neighbourhood. Even though Ma Jagadhartri has replaced the original, bloodthirsty Ma Kali, the goddess has not really left the temple. An inner shrine still houses a small bronze figure of the goddess.

The legends surrounding the temple and its deities have never been allowed to dwindle into obscurity. The town, after all, owes its existence to the temple. The town comes alive during the tourist season and the annual festival of Jagadhartri. Ahalya used to love the festivities, the fairs near the temple, and the crowds. Kanai used to love to watch her lose herself in that heady melee of people. But now Ahalya seems to love something else, and Kanai is no longer allowed to watch her.

The woman laughs again. Kanai sits up and looks about wildly. The laugh sounds familiar. He flees down the hill. But the thought that he is about to be haunted by something worse follows him all the way down.

Saroma corners him the following day. 'Kanai! You're not keeping an eye on her!'

He shuffles his feet, not daring to look at her.

'Kanai! Tell me! I know you're keeping something from me!' she hisses. 'Ahalya's my daughter. I can tell something's wrong with her. Kanai, please …'

'Saroma Mashi,' says Kanai, clearing his throat, 'Saroma Mashi, Ahalya's… She is old enough to be married, isn't she?'

'What are you trying to tell me, Kanai? Speak up!'

Kanai's heart thuds painfully against his ribcage. 'I can marry her, Saroma Mashi. I swear I can! Before it's too late.'

'What! You wretch!' Saroma spits the words out at

him. 'I'll break your legs. I'll pull out your tongue! Too late? What have you been doing to my Ahalya?'

'Saroma Mashi. Oh! Saroma Mashi!' Tears roll down Kanai cheeks. 'Please don't misunderstand me. Please, Mashi…'

But Saroma hurries into her house and slams the door shut.

Arati Mashi comes hobbling towards Kanai. 'Ki re Kanai, what's happened? Why are you crying?'

Kanai turns and walks away quickly. He hears Arati Mashi knocking on Saroma's door. Kanai is certain that Ahalya's days are numbered. She will be ostracized. Saroma Mashi will be shamed. This certainty weighs his shoulders down. He must find Ahalya, make a last plea. But the days walk past without even allowing him a glimpse of the girl.

~

Kanai continues to look for Ahalya. She does not go to the guesthouse these days. Haru Buro does not seem to have any clue about her whereabouts either. He is once again his usual, cantankerous self. Ahalya is nowhere to be found. Sometimes, Kanai believes, he can hear the unmistakable sound of her laughter when he passes by the temple. But that cannot be true. The priests would not tolerate a low-caste girl, however beautiful, inside their temple—would they?

Late one afternoon, Kanai creeps by Saroma's house. Snatches of a heated but whispered conversation float out. Arati Mashi and a few others like her are pressing against the house walls, too, straining their ears. When they spot him, they look at him with inquisitive eyes. The sun's baleful stare does not bother them. It bothers Kanai. He can feel the beginnings of a headache throbbing in his temples. But he is determined to get to Ahalya. Kanai slinks away to the rear of the house.

An open drain runs parallel to Saroma's house. Faeces, rotten food and ashes from coal stoves have all but choked the drain as it snakes its narrow way behind the row of houses. Kanai picks his way among the cats and stray dogs that always gather along the edges and climbs over the little wall with the wooden gate separating the drain from Saroma's house. He stands cowering under the latch of the back door, waiting for an opportunity.

He waits a long time. The sun is almost down when he finally musters up the courage to scratch lightly on the door. He pokes the door with his index finger. It creaks slightly and opens, just a little bit. Kanai is shocked. He pushes the door a little more, and then some more. He stands in the gloom, squinting to see clearly. Neither Saroma nor Ahalya have seen him enter.

'Saroma Mashi. Saroma Mashi,' he calls out softly, not daring to raise his voice.

Saroma peers at him. 'Kanai! How did you get in?'

'The back door was open Mashi, didn't you know?'

'Know? What do I know? Oh Kanai, the witch has ruined me…' Saroma's voice breaks down.

Kanai waits. He doesn't know what to say.

'I have not ruined anybody,' hisses Ahalya. Kanai can see her quite clearly now, leaning against the wall. 'I am getting married!'

Kanai's heart jumps at the words.

'Married! Married, she says! Girls like you who… who…do stupid things that no respectable girl would do can never get married,' sobs Saroma.

'He said he'd marry me. He said he'll take me to the city, and I will be happy there. What's there for me here anyway? I am sick of this stupid life here in this stupid place.'

'Keep quiet, shameless whore!' Saroma slaps Ahalya hard across the face. Kanai winces. Ahalya does not even flinch.

Saroma turns towards Kanai. 'Did you know all this? Did you know what she was doing all this time?'

'I… I wasn't sure. Mashi when I thought that things were getting out of hand, I… I tried to tell you… Mashi, I would never let Ahalya down.' Kanai trembles with emotion. 'Saroma Mashi, nobody need know anything more. I'll marry Ahalya; I'll marry her, Saroma Mashi. I will, no matter what!'

The two women look at him in silence, one in gratitude and the other in shock.

'Kanai, are you sure?' Saroma walks softly towards him. 'Are you sure of what you're saying? I am a very poor woman, Kanai. And, after all that's happened, you still want…'

'Yes, Saroma Mashi, yes, yes! It makes no difference to me. None of it.'

'I misjudged you Kanai,' says Saroma. 'I had not imagined…' But the rest of her words are cut off by a short crisp laugh.

Saroma spins around as if she has been stung. Kanai stares at Ahalya. Her hair floats around her face in waves of black rebellion. Her eyes go dark with passion.

'Marry me! Oh. He wants to marry me! Oh! My saintly goatherd!' Ahalya shoves both Saroma and Kanai out of the way as she lets herself out the back door.

'Stop her! Oh stop that wretch,' screams Saroma.

Her scream is immediately followed by a pounding on her front door, Arati Mashi and her friends have waited long enough, and now they want in. There is nothing to be done. Both doors are open. Ahalya is lost through one, beyond Kanai's reach. And the women of the neigbourhood pour in through the other.

They spend the night searching for her among the hills, with hurricane lamps to light their way. The men from Ahalya's locality grill Haru Buro while the women

question his wife. The sahari babus are gone and even
beating old Haru does not yield any clue. They prowl
around the temple walls until the priests come out to
curse them. Some of them even walk to the little railway
station at the other end of town. Still nothing. Saroma
weeps continuously. The women try to comfort her as
best as they can. But their words cut her like whiplashes.
They cannot get her to eat. For days afterwards, Saroma
roams the hills like a mad woman, searching. Long after
everybody has given up hope, every rumour brings
Saroma running out. She does not mind the gossip any
more. She has nothing left to lose.

Months pass. Ahalya's misdeeds become afternoon
gossip. The sahari babus do not return to sketch the
temple. Mothers are relieved, but they never stop warning
their daughters of the consequences of mixing with bad
men from the cities. Stray rumours still circulate, and
add fuel to the terror in mothers' hearts. Some tell how
Ahalya was running up the hill to her lover when the
dreaded goddess pulled her into the earth by her hair;
others tell of a band of roaming tantrics which sacrificed
her; yet others whisper that Ahalya was murdered after
she refused her lover's offer of money, and insisted that
he marry her. Old Shibu at the ration shop claims that
his mother's cousin-brother's son-in-law's friend saw a
dancing girl who looked like Ahalya entertaining a group
of drunkards. Someone else says that a beggar woman

looking suspiciously like Ahalya was last seen at a nearby railway station. The stories continue. Saroma seems to live for these stories, whether they are true or not, and for the sympathy of her neighbours. But Kanai stays away from the stories. And he still searches for Ahalya, hoping against hope that she will turn up someday, somehow.

The months roll into years. And the years pick their way through time, single file. Ahalya's story gets buried in the dump yard of old gossip. Ahalya's name no longer has the power to frighten the little girls of the town into submission. The town itself grows thin as the younger denizens leave to find better lives in the cities, and then grows fat again as new people move in from the surrounding villages. Saroma is dead. She died clutching her bitterness like a quilt to her heart. Kanai lit her funeral pyre and it is he who now lives in her house.

Kanai works at the railway station, doing odd jobs for the stationmaster. He is married with children of his own, fiercely loyal to his family, and excessively protective about his daughters. His wife is a little afraid of his ways, and does not demand more than he feels obligated to give her.

The sahari babus who had stopped coming have returned again. Except that these new babus are a new breed altogether. Some of them are not even babus, but serious bespectacled women in jeans who paint ferociously within the temple precincts, detailing the architectural nuances on their canvas with a sharpness that defies photography. The temple though, stands like an eternal monument, unabashed by the wear and tear on its façade. The number of priests has dwindled. The lamps have diminished. The sound of the priests' chanting has receded into echoes. The crowd of worshippers has grown sparse. Then, one day, something happens that promises the return of old glory.

'A miracle has occurred!' gushes the head priest. 'The goddess has spoken. Oh a miracle. A miracle!'

The news spreads like wild fire. The entire town rushes to the temple. People pour in from everywhere, even though the annual festival of Jagadhartri and the tourist season is still a month away. The little town begins to bear a festive air. Special prayer services are held almost daily. Vendors gather around the temple, selling all kinds of things from puja offerings to sweets, toys and balloons.

Kanai's community is also caught up in the excitement. They have not yet seen the miracle, but have heard of a new black clay deity that has sprung up near the inner shrine. The temple priests, in a rare gesture of generosity, have promised to let them have a glimpse if they, the untouchables, can hoist themselves up on the walls of the temple. Hundreds have begun to throng the temple grounds.

Everyone is talking about the new deity. Kanai is

curious too. So he goes along with his family. He finds a good place for himself and his wife, and hoists the children on the lower branch of a shaggy pipul tree just outside the wall. His wife passes up salted peanuts and roasted gram to her children. She is hopeful that after catching a glimpse of the new deity, Kanai will take them to the impromptu fair that has sprung up on the hillside.

They gaze in wonder at the deity, glistening black, freshly sprung from the innards of the hill. The deity's head is thrown back and looking upwards. Snake-like ropes of black clay uncoil in a petrified cascade down her back and reach below the waist. Black breasts heave like a pair of frozen peaks. Two arms are extended as if in supplication. She stands there as if cast in the very clay she had been trying desperately to shake free. Priests start to chant and the worshipers walk up to touch the deity. The line of worshippers is more than a mile long, winding round and round, until it covers the whole of the temple grounds.

Kanai too gazes, but neither in wonder nor reverence. Old sorrows and a half digested lump of anguish heaves in his breast. The pain grows intolerable after a while and the bitter tears roll down his cheeks. He knows her. How can he not? Has he not been carrying her inside him like a touchstone all these years? How can he not recognize this new deity for who she really is, when the fresh memory of her face touches him into wakefulness every morning and squeezes back into his innards every time he does his husbandly duty towards his wife? Kanai trembles. The pain stabs his heart and whips his loins. Watching the terrible emotions chasing around Kanai's face, his wife too weeps, quietly into the edge of her sari. No one must see her shame, and the farce of her marriage. It is all clear to her now—her husband's moody silences, the echoes of the past ululating through the lips of the women on their wedding day, the whispers behind her back. It is as fresh as the deity that stands before them now, glistening beneath the sun, defying nature, defying time, defying convention.

Hijras on the Highway

Patwari drained his glass of extra sweet masala tea and lit a bidi. He squinted as he inhaled. The setting sun shone like polished brass. The Durga Puja festival was still a couple of weeks away, but the town had already started to behave as if the holidays had begun. Patwari felt happy, perhaps because it was still light, though fast fading. He liked to enjoy his afternoons: a short nap after lunch followed by a glass of kadak chai and a smoke when the sun hovered on the horizon. He was never in a hurry to get started. The bustle would begin at seven after Sardarji arrived.

Sardarji's real name was Gurdeep Singh Bhattal, but to all at the bus depot he was known as Sardarji. Physically, he fit the stereotype: six feet tall, muscle-bound and strong, a twirling moustache and a rich beard which clasped his jaw, piercing black eyes and a loud guffaw. Sardarji had a sardar's temper, too. He was not easily angered but when roused, his roar could put tigers to shame and his blows could crush an elephant's skull. At least that was what Patwari liked to claim.

Patwari was the opposite of Sardarji, a puny man, all skin and bone. But his physical deficiencies had never stopped him from getting into fights. Sardarji always said that Patwari's acid tongue and ill-timed sense of humour would bring them bad trouble one day. Nevertheless, Patwari and Sardarji got along famously. This was partly because Patwari didn't unleash his sense of humour on his friend. On his part, Sardarji felt protective towards Patwari. But their friendship thrived mostly because the two men had been together for a very long time and made a good team. Sardarji drove the mini bus from the Asansol bus depot to Ranchi and back every day. Patwari was the bus conductor.

'Ho Patwari. Sat Sri Akal!' Sardarji strode into the depot and gave the bus a friendly slap.

'Sat Sri Akal, Sardarji!' Patwari raised his bidi in a salute before flinging it across the dusty tarmac with his thumb and index finger. He got up, cracked his knuckles, and stretched. Another Asansol-Ranchi-Asansol roundtrip had begun.

The passengers started to trickle in at a quarter to seven. Patwari eyed them idly. Most of them had already bought their tickets at the booth in the depot, so he didn't bother to get up. He would check their tickets at leisure once the bus started. Besides, from his years of experience as a bus conductor, he could tell a ticketless traveller from ten yards away. They rarely had that problem. This was a long-distance route, frequented mostly by families and middle-aged businessmen. College kids also took the route at the start and the finish of their academic terms. But these young people, though boisterous, never gave them any trouble. On the other hand, some of the family men would sometimes try to palm off a buxom girl or a gangly youth as a minor just to save half the cost of a ticket.

Once Patwari disgustedly told the father of a giggly young lady that she was old enough to bear his— Patwari's—children, and Sardarji had to intervene and break up the ugly scene that followed. Patwari was made to apologize for being disrespectful, but not before the father's pride had crumbled before Sardarji's flexed muscles.

Today's passengers were almost exclusively of the family type, except for an unshaven student who seemed to be returning to Ranchi after a weekend jaunt. A few other passengers caught Patwari's eye. Among them were four Gujaratis, middle-aged couples who appeared to be either very intimate friends or relatives on good terms with each other. The foursome sat together in the only two seats that faced each other in the bus, mumbling softly like a covey of partridges. A couple of seats away sat an old mullah with a young woman and her infant. The woman looked frail and sick, and her baby was so small that it was barely visible through the sheets and towels swaddling it. A broad Hindu matriarch with her husband, sister-in-law, and brother-in-law presided over the seats in the middle. The rest of the seats were occupied by single gentlemen travelling to Ranchi on business and young couples engrossed in themselves.

The bus hummed into life at seven-thirty sharp. It was dark by then, and the passengers shifted restlessly in the dim halo of the bus-lights. Sardarji gave his moustache a twirl, which was Patwari's signal to sing out, 'Chal sawari!' and slap the side of the bus, balancing on the steps with the door half-closed. He would continue to lean out of the door until the bus gathered speed and left the town for the highway. He would then leave his post by the steps and check the passengers' tickets, sometimes making conversation with those who felt inclined to talk. At last Sardarji would make eye contact with him in the rear-view mirror, signalling that it was time for Patwari to produce the tobacco pouch and roll out two cigarettes. And Patwari would oblige, rolling them carefully, seated on the foam-covered bench on the left of the driver's seat, across the gearbox and engine. He would light both cigarettes and hand one over to Sardarji.

They would smoke and indulge in small talk, and sometimes the passengers, at least those who were seated in front and close enough to hear above the roar of the bus's engine would join in as well. Smoking hand-rolled cigarettes was a luxury Patwari enjoyed but could not really afford. Sardarji knew this, and he did not smoke more than one or two per trip. Sometimes Sardarji would buy a pouch of tobacco and casually leave it on the bench. Patwari never acknowledged it, but Sardarji knew that his gift was appreciated.

The bus travelled along the Grand Trunk Road leading towards Dhanbad, gathering speed with every milestone it crossed. They would reach Dhanbad at around nine in the night and stop there for about forty minutes while the passengers stretched and ate some light tiffin in lieu of dinner. Patwari and Sardarji would refuel there, themselves as well as the bus. There was a particular tea shop they patronized, into which the bus passengers sometimes followed. This time it was the old mullah and the woman with her baby who joined them.

The old man ordered tea for himself and puri-bhaji for the young woman. She seemed to be ill at ease with the baby, which started to cry. The baby's cries created a din in the gloomy and otherwise quiet tea shop. Patwari turned around to say something but Sardarji stopped him. The noise had attracted two hijras. They sidled into the shop, clicking their tongues and clapping their hands. The woman cringed and held her baby close. The old mullah stood up in agitation.

'Arre Daddu! Why are you worried? Don't you want us to bless the child?' lisped one of the hijras, swinging her false braid. 'We'll bring you good luck,' sang the other, eyeing the woman. Their presence should have been auspicious; however, in this case, it turned out to be otherwise.

The old mullah turned almost hysterical at the mention of good luck. 'What good luck? Look at my poor daughter. She's been turned out from her husband's home because of this baby! Those scoundrels questioned my daughter's virtue. Good luck? Never have I met one as unlucky as my poor daughter!'

The young woman tried to hush her father. Her baby, sensing trouble, stopped bawling and quietened down into a soft whimper. Rocking the infant in her arms and trying to comfort the old man at the same time, the frail young woman cut a poignant picture. Patwari spoke up, 'Oye hijre saale! Get out of here or I will kick you!'

'Ye, ei! Babu! Who's talking to you?' The hijras turned towards Patwari. Being bigger built, they towered over the smaller man until Sardarji stood up.

'You are talking to my passengers,' Sardarji said quietly. The hijras looked at him for a couple of seconds, then turned and left, muttering among themselves.

Patwari and Sardarji returned to their tea but were interrupted again. This time it was the news and crowds of curious people materialized before the radios and TVs in every shop on that road. As soon as the gist of the news had been digested, opinions were formed. People excitedly discussed the World Trade Centre and the forces that had brought it down, though nobody among them had seen the towers. The two men also listened. It took them a little while to unravel the sequence of events and the number of lives lost. The name Osama Bin Laden ricocheted around the walls and then zoomed in again to buzz in the ears of the people. Nobody was sure about Bin Laden's identity at first. But as is the case, there is always some truly wise guy who knows all about everything. Such a person quickly gathers a following when rapid news is required, and his knowledge spreads through the ranks. The two gentlemen among the Gujarati foursome turned out to be the most knowledgeable and garrulous. They had already gathered a small crowd at the Madras Tiffin House a few shops away from Patwari and Sardarji's tea shop. And when they boarded, the bus suddenly became an unlikely soapbox for the duo's oratorical skills.

Sardarji started the bus amidst the hubbub without remembering to twirl his moustache. And Patwari didn't loiter at the steps after shouting, 'Chal sawari!' The passengers of the Asansol-Ranchi-Asansol roundtrip mini bus had returned to their seats enlightened and excited after their halt at Dhanbad. They felt a heightened sense of the world around them, its past and present, and the powers that be, both good and evil, that could change destinies forever. They naturally drew parallels with the tragedies in New York and their own knowledge of what had been occurring in India. The whole bus became a movable feast of opinions that were ladled back and forth, forth and back. Anecdotal history dotted discussions of world and Indian politics, and the whys and wherefores were discussed animatedly.

The atmosphere in the bus became increasingly charged, and Patwari was eager to participate. 'So mian saab,' said Patwari, grinning widely at the old mullah, 'this Bin Laden fellow is from your religion…'

The old man looked up at him with a puzzled frown. But the sudden lull in the conversation gave him inkling that this piece of wit was misplaced, and his face became immediately stern. 'Arre bhai? What are you saying?' said the mullah. 'Is this the way to joke with an old man?'

Patwari sensed the change in the atmosphere and smiled sheepishly. 'No offence, mian saab. Just joking.'

Sardarji scowled at him in the rear-view mirror. But the atmosphere had grown considerably chilly, and even the bus tyres seemed to whisper, 'Muslim, Muslim, Muslim.'

It dawned on the old man that he, his daughter, and the baby were the only Muslims in the bus. He looked away and tried to busy himself with the baby and his daughter. But the cloud of sudden suspicion and hostility grew thick behind his back. Whispers rose higher and higher and marooned the little Muslim family in their corner of the bus. Sardarji concentrated on the road ahead, and Patwari sat on his seat counting coins. The lights from houses and shops on the sides of the highway grew sparser as they sped away from Dhanbad, until it was just the speeding lights from passing vehicles and their bus on the dark road.

An hour later, the bus limped to a stop; one of its tyres had been punctured. Sardarji cursed. Changing a bus-tyre in the middle of the highway, with only a torch to see by was a painful and time-consuming affair. Patwari got down from the bus to take the spare tyre out. The passengers, who had begun to nod off, became suddenly fully awake and hostile again. They frowned at the trio as if they were to blame for the puncture. Many of the passengers decided to stretch their limbs on the dusty footpath flanking the road, and the old man urged his daughter to do so too, as the baby had grown listless in the bus. She obeyed, only to walk straight into the arms of trouble.

A few dilapidated buildings, long abandoned by their original owners, hugged the edge of the road. Kerosene lamps glowed from nooks, and gave the place a spooky appearance. Hijras lived here, plying their trade for truckers who preferred more exotic fare over the women who serviced them on the highways. It was from here that the hijras made their regular forays into the town and back, hitching rides on buses and trucks several times a day. The young woman was unfortunate that two of the hijras who emerged from the buildings happened to be the same ones who had heckled her and her father at the tea shop earlier that evening. Emboldened by the presence of their sisters, they were now more than ready to lay siege.

'All right mian saab. Now let's see how you wriggle out of this,' said the one who lisped. And immediately a chorus followed. The mullah tried to bundle his daughter back onto the bus, but she was too petrified to move. One of the hijras snatched the baby from her arms and examined it. The mother let out a wail of terror that was immediately echoed by her baby. The bus passengers stood shocked and silent by this display of aggression.

'Oye!' shouted Patwari. 'You give the baby back to the mother!'

'Hai!' shouted the hijras back. 'Hai. Hai. We won't. What will you do, re?'

'Ei conductor,' said the lisper's partner, clapping his hands menacingly. 'You were such a hero back there. Now let's see you get your two fathers here, haanh!'

'Sardarji!' shrieked Patwari.

'Sardarji!' mimicked the hijras, drowning out the mother's wails with their clapping.

Sardarji brought himself up to his full height and advanced, glaring at the hijras. The hijras looked at him and laughed. They lifted their skirts up to their knees.

'Oye Sardarji! Want to have a good time? Come see what's under our skirts!'

This was too much for Sardarji, and he fled to the rear of the bus where the punctured tyre awaited his muscles.

The other passengers also fled to the relative safety of the bus and craned through the windows to get a better glimpse of the drama outside. They could make out the old man and his daughter from their silhouettes. But Patwari seemed to be lost among the many gesticulating limbs and bobbing heads. They heard the old man cry out, 'Please, sirs, help us. Please, they've taken my grandson away. Oh please, don't be so hard hearted.'

'Give us two hundred rupees and you can take your child!' screamed the hijras. 'Hey hero,' they said to Patwari, 'why don't you get the money?'

Patwari spat on the dust but otherwise held his peace. Some of the bus passengers shouted out to the old man, urging him to give the hijras the money and avoid further harassment.

'Brothers, where will a poor person like me get two hundred rupees to spare?' he cried. And turning to the hijras, he said, 'Oh sisters, what harm have we done to you? You can see how wretched we already are. Can you not be a little kind? Please, Allah will bless you.'

The hijras were not to be deprived of their two hundred rupees. Their pride had been injured at the teashop, and now that they had the old man cornered, they had no intention of letting go. The passengers, too, didn't seem inclined to help. Many of them had started to show impatience. Sardarji got the new tyre in place, but didn't walk up to the hijras. He quietly got into the driver's seat and waited. The passengers asked him to negotiate. Sardarji shook his head and sat tight behind the wheel. He didn't like the idea of having his manhood compromised by a bunch of non-women. This was the same predicament for all the male passengers in the bus, even though it was their duty to protect. But who wanted to exchange words with shameless hijras that lifted up their skirts at the drop of a hat? Patwari first inched towards the bus but changed his mind and turned towards the old man. He looked at the rest of the passengers. 'Arre bhaiyon, stand with me. Let's fix this.'

'Arre bhaiyon!' mimicked the hijras. 'Come come, we'll show you what's underneath our skirts!'

Nobody moved. The young woman kept stretching her arms towards the baby, but she didn't dare go up to the hijras. She didn't notice that her baby was actually gurgling cheerfully in the arms of an older hijra who was holding the child in her arms like a tender flower. Her face exuded kindness and affection. The rest of the people were too excited at the prospect of a showdown to care about anything else. The stalemate showed no signs of abating. A crowd of curious villagers had gathered; they pointed and gesticulated but kept a safe distance.

The once vociferous Gujarati gentlemen were absolutely silent inside the bus. They even kept their eyes averted from the drama outside. The two Gujarati ladies showed concern and whispered to each other agitatedly. The young couples were quiet and watched everything with round eyes, shocked by this rude intrusion into their private world. The solitary gentlemen remained as they were, solitary and silent. The student slept with his head on the window on the side facing away from the hijras. But the matriarch was beginning to lose patience. She was a big woman, and used to having her way. Her gold bangles jangled angrily. She nudged her husband, but he didn't respond. She looked at all the other women sitting docilely next to their husbands, and snorted. Then she got up.

'Are we mothers or what?' demanded the matriarch. 'What is this nonsense? How can we sit here and allow strangers to snatch her child? Isn't she a mother like us? Muslim or not, she is a mother, right?' The women nodded and murmured. Taking this to be a sign of courage, the matriarch got up and pushed her way into the aisle of the bus. She turned to the other women, 'Come, sisters, let's show the men how we deal with such situations!'

What followed was a lengthy discussion in murmurs and sometimes raucous disagreement. The old man stood on the outer edges of the group, wringing his hands. Patwari stood next to him, looking sheepish. Finally the matriarch called out to him. Patwari edged forward. She motioned him to collect money from the men in the bus, which Patwari, grateful to play a positive role at last, proceeded to do with energy. Sardarji gave two twenty-rupee notes, signalling that it was from both of them. Patwari accepted with a salute. The other passengers, except for the student who slept on, quietly contributed their tens and twenties. The matriarch handed over the collection to one of the ladies to count, away from the hijras' curious eyes. Some further exchanges followed, after which the baby was handed over to his mother who was near fainting. The matriarch and older hijra exchanged friendly good-byes. The younger hijras winked at the men in the bus, and one of them gave Patwari a friendly prod, which he accepted, grinning. And the bus was ready to start.

The matriarch returned to her seat and shot a triumphant look at her husband and all the men around her. Some of the men had the grace to thank her for easing them out of a sticky situation. The rest of the women, too, felt pleased with themselves, and soon began a friendly discussion with the young mother about her baby and her circumstances. This last friendly gesture was enough to get the old man started, and he poured out his tale of woe to all sympathetic ears. Soon the baby was passed around from lap to lap and crooned over. Snacks were offered to the mother and the old man. The passengers lapsed into easy affability as the bus rolled on towards Ranchi.

Patwari lit two cigarettes and offered one to Sardarji. The sardar took it and said, 'Saala, next time don't expect me to bail you out!'

Patwari said nothing. He simply bent his head and inhaled deeply.

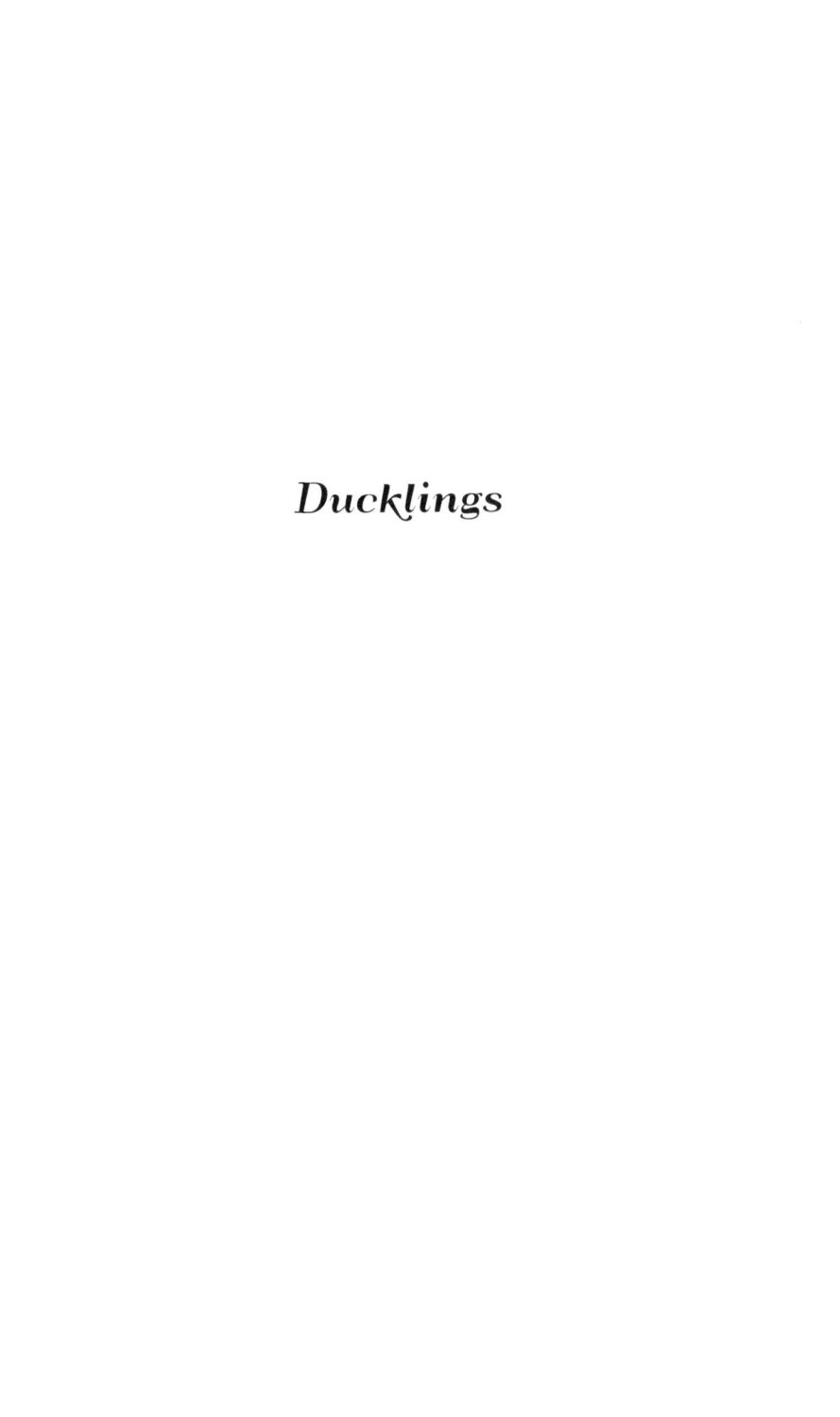

Ducklings

'Shiuli!' called out Nityananda as he peered into the dark. The pre-dawn air was chilly even though winter was months away. He hunched his shoulders and drew the threadbare shawl tighter around him. Shivering as he rubbed his elbows to increase circulation, Nityananda wondered how many more seasons his old bones would take. He had been more of a father than a doting grandfather to the children for so long, when he could have sat in the sun like his friends. His duties were far from over though. He prayed that god would let him live long enough to see Shiuli married and Laltu and Poltu settled.

'Shiuli! O Shiuli!' he called out once more but the girl was nowhere to be seen. She must have gone off to the pond to be with her precious ducklings. Ever since they have hatched, Shiuli, Laltu and Poltu have gone berserk, he thought in exasperation. It was not as if these were the first ducklings they had seen. Their mothers, grandmothers and great grandmothers had hatched in the pen near the pond. Along with a couple of generations of goats and calves as well. Generations of chickens had hatched and grown up and gone to market before the ducklings. Just like the ducks and the goats before them. He had half a mind to go there and drag her back.

A fluffy yellow ball quacked at him questioningly before skittering off towards the pond. Nityananda found himself smiling. Who could resist the innocence of these creatures? Especially Shuili, and they followed her wherever she went. Shiuli was a born mother, thought Nityananda fondly. Then he stopped. A deep frown appeared on his forehead. Their lot was a hard one. The earlier Shiuli learnt the truth the better it would be for all of them. It would be cruel of him, no doubt, to break her heart. But she would have to learn to bear that too.

Shiuli was eighteen and, under happier circumstances, might have been married. She might even have had a child or two. But losing both parents to cholera in a span of just four weeks had transformed Shiuli into a surrogate mother for her two younger brothers at the tender age of twelve. The boys, twins, had been four years old at that time. Shuili's three other siblings had also perished in the epidemic that had swept through their whole district. Nityananda knew he was lucky. God had been merciful and spared his three grandchildren when he could have taken them all in one fell swoop. Still, he rued his fate. He wished that he had died instead of his son and daughter-in-law. God was cruel. Why else would able-bodied young people like his daughter-in-law and son die instead of an old man like him? Why would small farmers like them, who were barely able to eke out a living from the few animals and the little land they owned, be assaulted by this sudden scourge? Nityananda leaned against the mud wall of his home. It was not just the economic disaster looming before him; they had seen worse and would survive. His grandchildren had never faced a situation like this before. Their hearts had not grown the callouses that Nityananda's had. Watching them with the ducklings caused him more pain than he cared to show.

Shiuli had wanted to study. From the time she could hold a slate and chalk, she had followed her grandfather about repeating the letters of the alphabet and writing them down after Nityananda had scratched them out on the dry soil. Shiuli never let go until she had fully grasped her lesson for the day. By the time she was seven, she could add or subtract numbers in her head and write full sentences. Haripada, Shiuli's father, used to be proud of his clever daughter. 'Shiuli will be a teacher,' Haripada would say, picking her up and swinging her above his broad shoulders. 'Every time our Shiuli walks past adjusting her spectacles and brandishing her ruler, everybody in the village will say, "Namoshkar Mashtarni Didimoni, namoshkar!"'

Shiuli would giggle delightedly. Nityananda would add with a twinkle in his eyes, 'But our Mashtarni Didimoni will say namoshkar to me with folded hands every time she leaves for school, because I was her first teacher!' And Shiuli would promptly swing towards her dadu, her darling grandfather, and grab his arms.

Yes, they had many dreams for Shiuli, dreams that were as sweet as the jasmine that scented their garden in summer. They would lie down under the stars and talk about Shiuli's future even as Madhobi, Nityananda's daughter-in-law, would grumble under her breath that the rightful place for a girl was in her husband's house and Shiuli was better off learning to cook and clean instead of getting her head filled with frivolous ideas. Shiuli's mother had her reasons. Neighbours often passed snide remarks about Haripada's and Nityananda's dreams. Besides, girl children were normally never allowed to finish school in the village. It was not the custom. The village elders disapproved of so much attention being paid to girls. They frowned upon girls gallivanting around after puberty. The earlier you married off a girl the better it was. Nityananda had himself brought Madhobi home when she was barely fourteen and practically illiterate, but well versed in household duties and an expert cook. She was only twenty-eight when, weakened by multiple pregnancies and miscarriages, she succumbed to the cholera epidemic. Haripada did not get a chance to mourn his wife for long. He followed some weeks later, after watching three of his children writhe in pain and die, one after the other.

~

Nityananda dabbed at the tears that pricked the corners of his rheumy eyes and trickled down. He went in to wake up the boys.

As part of their morning routine, Laltu and Poltu would help him feed their cow and two goats. Meanwhile, Shiuli would feed the chickens and the ducks. It was only after the animals had been fed that they would eat their breakfast of puffed rice soaked in tea. This family routine had been fixed at the children's insistence. They could never bear to eat until all their four-legged and winged family members had had their fill. The three children's world revolved around these mute creatures who demanded their love. And who, in turn, gave back in full measure with their nuzzling and cooing and clucking, and by following the members of the family about whenever they happened to be nearby. Shiuli always spoke to all the animals as if they were her own babies—the ducklings were of course her favourites. Not only because they were the youngest members of Nityananda's household, but because they were as motherless as Shiuli, Laltu and Poltu, a jackal having carried off their mother soon after they had hatched. Nityananda understood. It did not help him though.

Nityananda was a practical and life-hardened man. His own behaviour towards the animals was gruff. Not that it made any difference as far as the animals were concerned. They would still go up to him and follow him around whenever he was near. Nityananda would scold them even as he stroked the larger animals or threw a handful of puffed rice at the chickens and ducks. Nityananda knew only too well that attachment created problems. Like that time he had to sell the year-old pie-bald male kid to the butcher and Laltu and Poltu had cried for days. Shiuli had consoled them and given him black looks. Nityananda had ignored them. She would never know how bad he had felt that day; as if he had sold his own grandson. But he had had to do it. What choice did he have? Someday, when they were grown up, they would understand.

Nityananda crossed the narrow courtyard that separated his room from that of the boys. He bent his head to avoid the strands of thatch hanging over the low doorway. He didn't like to wake the boys up so early. They were so young; if they didn't play and read and have fun now, when would they ever?

'Time flows like a river and never stops for even a moment,' muttered Nityananda to himself. Soon the boys would be lost to manhood. The pleasures of running down a field and splashing in the pond would be lost to them. The magic of a new world unfolding day by day would be gone forever.

Laltu and Poltu attended the government primary school. Every day, before they left in the morning, they would help Nityananda with the cow and the goats. Together, they would untie the animals and lead them out down the village road. Once they reached a customer's house, either Laltu or Poltu would call out while Nityananda sat down on his haunches to milk the cow. The boys were quite adept at milking the goats, but Nityananda still preferred to milk the cow himself. He would measure and pour the milk from the pail into the vessel that his customer handed over. Laltu would collect the money or note the amount due in a notebook. After that they would move on to the next house and then to the next, until all their customers were served. This was a slow and sometimes tedious process. It would have been better for Nityananda's old bones if the boys took the milk to their customers later in the day. Raw milk didn't go bad if you kept strips of straw in the cans. But people liked to buy milk that they could watch being milked straight from the cow. So Laltu and Poltu had to be woken up at the crack of dawn, even during holidays. Today, however, they seemed to have gotten up on their own. Nityananda rubbed his eyes and looked again. The straw mats that served as their beds were empty.

'Shiuli! O Shiuli! Laltu! Poltu! Where are you?'

No one answered.

Alarmed all at once, Nityananda hurried out. He

looked to the right and left and then went down to the pond. In the pale morning light he was able to make out shadowy shapes huddled near the pond steps. He called out again. The shapes remained still. A broken sob caught his ears. Nityananda ran towards the sound.

He found them sitting there, hugging the ducklings. Shiuli was crying her heart out. Laltu and Poltu were crying, and trying to comfort their sister at the same time. Shiuli, bent over with grief, sat holding the ducklings to her bosom. Shiuli, sobbing as if she were about to lose her own children. Shiuli, who no longer ran up numbers inside her head or read fluently from the day-old newspaper that Nityananda sometimes brought home from the village school-master's house. Shiuli, who had grown day by day into an exact replica of her mother, and turned into a quiet dutiful woman, a good cook and a devoted home-maker.

Nityananda stood there taking it all in, and felt his heart cracking under the weight of sorrow. His eyes stung, but the tears remained unshed. He wished he could weep like the children. He ached to hold the half-grown ducklings to his bosom and shower them with kisses. But what was the use of getting emotional? He was helpless. There was no way he could save the ducklings. This was the stone-hard truth that he alone had to swallow. Perhaps some day his grandchildren would understand. Perhaps they never would, and would always grudge him his gruff ways.

Nityananda shut his eyes. He felt the darkness close around him. He would not look at the ducklings. Instead he would look at the empty pens and ponds in their village. All the places this wretched bird flu had struck. He would look into the eyes of the men in white suits who would be coming over to claim the little ones, as well as all the other fowls in th neighbourhood, any day now. And he would not shed tears for them. Just like he had not for Haripada, Madhabi and his dead grandchildren.

The Vanishing Man

Satyabrata Chatterjee looked at his old Favre Leuba watch. He had received it as a wedding gift from his wife's parents. There were brown spots on the dial. A cheap faux leather strap had long replaced the original. But it had never occurred to Satyabrata to replace the timepiece. It had been with him during those first heady days of marriage, and had served him faithfully through the routine of life thereafter: the birth of his children and the slow, steady rise up the ranks of clerkdom. Satyabrata looked at his watch in the coppery light of the setting sun and drew in a long slow breath.

Today was his last day at work. Rather, it had been his last day, for the working hours had ended. His colleagues had bidden him farewell during the lunch hour. Satyabrata's farewell gifts were neatly stacked on his otherwise empty table. There would be plenty of time to open and look at them at home.

Satyabrata was looking forward to his new life. He would get up later than usual and linger over his morning tea. He would leisurely read the newspaper and haggle more tenaciously with the fishmonger. Yes, he would miss his old routine, he mused. That was but natural. He would miss the smell of starched cotton shirts laid out on the bed in the mornings. The scent of Cantheridine hair oil on his fingertips after he had run them through his still damp hair. He would no longer need to shine his shoes, but he would still run a brush over them for old time's sake, he thought. Just because he had retired didn't mean he had to let himself go to seed. But first things first, he would buy some of the things that he had put on hold for a long time, now that he had the money. On the advice of his eldest son Debabrata, Debu, Satyabrata had not opted for the pension scheme. Instead, he had chosen to take his provident fund and pension together. The thought of all that money sitting in his bank account made Satyabrata feel rich and generous.

At the top of his list was a pair of diamond earrings for Urmilla. She had long wanted a little something. Urmilla had never been a nagging wife. But she had a way of sighing that used to almost break his heart when they were first married, though that feeling had given way to helplessness and even impatience as the years went by. Still, as her husband and her provider, Satyabrata had always tried to fulfill her wishes. Urmilla, on her part, had borne him two sons and a daughter, cooked decent meals and occasionally massaged his back and legs. She was a good wife and Satyabrata felt that he could and ought to indulge her, even if it made a dent in his retirement money.

'Satya-da? Still here?' said Manoj.

Manoj was the office peon whose many duties included bringing tea for the clerks and other babus and sweeping the office after and before work hours.

'Feeling sad, Satya-da?'

Satyabrata got up, smiling genially. The thought occurred to him now, looking at Manoj's friendly, enquiring face, that his colleagues and superiors had not been showing much interest in him lately. They had also gone through the motions of his farewell in a distant, polite sort of way. Satyabrata did not mind. He had not really expected them to be emotional about his departure. He was just one among dozens of senior clerks doing the same work day after day, year after year, until the faces of his reporting officers, one replacing the other, blurred into an unrecognizable yet familiar face and he no longer cared who he reported to.

'Sad? Not at all,' said Satyabrata. 'I am a grandfather now! It's time I stopped working and played with my little dadubhai.'

'Ah, yes, yes, you are right Satya-da,' said Manoj. 'If only I was as fortunate as you. But what can a man like me do? Look at me. I am past retirement age but I have to work. My sons are useless. My wife is almost bedridden. My daughter ran away with a scoundrel…'

Manoj's voice took on a wheedling tone. Everybody in the office knew about Manoj's troubles. He always had a tale or two of woe for any babu he managed to corner. The babus put up with it because Manoj was the most indispensable person in the office. Without Manoj to bring in the tea every mid-morning and afternoon, they would have died of thirst; and the office would have collapsed had Manoj not been there to constantly ferry the files and papers back and forth. Today, however, Satyabrata felt he could dispense with that obligation. Instead of encouraging Manoj with a kindly 'hmm', he frowned, gathered up his presents and long black umbrella with impatient hands, and started towards the door.

Manoj, sensing Satyabrata's impatience, hurried after him. 'Satya-da?' he simpered. 'You won't forget us now, will you? You will remember this poor brother of yours?'

Satyabrata relented. A little lump of sentiment bobbed up inside his throat. He had worked here for forty years; in fact, he was one of the oldest employees, and now, on his last day at work, Manoj was the only one who seemed sad to see him go. But that was how people were. They only cared about you as long as you were of use. To each his own gain, Satyabrata thought philosophically. He patted Manoj's shoulder.

'I am a free man now Manoj! Free to indulge my memory however I want. But will *you* remember me?'

'Oh, yes, of course Satya-da,' said Manoj, clutching Satyabrata's hand eagerly.

Satyabrata smiled. Perhaps Manoj was asking for a little baksheesh. Well, he was not going to get it. He had no business wheedling money out of a retired man. A thin curl of disdain crept into Satyabrata's smile, which Manoj either did not notice or pretended not to.

~

Satyabrata spent the first few weeks of his retirement doing all the things he had planned to do. He went for leisurely morning walks. He poured tea into a saucer and sipped it with relish as he read the newspaper. He took long naps in the afternoon. And he played with his year-old grandson. He hummed as he combed his hair and sniffed his fingertips afterwards. He took to wearing dhotis, and admired their pristine whiteness underneath cream-coloured kurtas. Urmilla joked that he looked like a bridegroom. He certainly felt like one these days!

Urmilla was almost delirious with happiness with her diamond earrings. Sonali, their daughter-in-law, did not look too pleased. Satyabrata saw her whispering to Debu. This was only a small cloud in his sky. Nothing could mar his holiday mood.

Satyabrata started to take a keen interest in the house after the initial euphoria wore off. He discovered cracks and leaks that needed mending. The house also needed a fresh coat of paint, and a new set of curtains. Unlike in the past, Satyabrata felt that he could start immediately, instead of waiting for the Puja bonus. It was not such a bad idea to get the house spruced up now; he would soon be looking for a bride for his younger son.

Shaktibrata, Shakti, had found a decent job with the Indian Railways. He was still a long way away from becoming a stationmaster, but it was a good start. Satyabrata had heard that railway employees could earn a lot of unaccounted-for money. If Shakti played his cards right, who knew, he might even start earning more than Debu, who, by virtue of his good academic result, was a bank officer. That would cut Sonali down to size. She had been acting snooty with him lately.

As these pleasant thoughts ran through his mind, Satyabrata felt refreshed, even a little young. He took his empty cup to Urmilla for a refill.

Urmilla was cooking lunch. She did the cooking even though they had Sonali. Satyabrata assumed that she preferred to do it. He was glad that she did. Satyabrata did not relish Sonali's cooking, though Debu seemed pleased enough with it. Satyabrata put his cup down next to Urmilla, where she was squatting near the stove. The bonthi lay on its side close to her, and a mound of cut vegetables rested in a large wicker basket next to it. Satyabrata did not have to say anything. He knew that Urmilla would notice the cup and quickly make him more tea, even if it meant taking the pot off the stove. The diamonds in her ears, despite being as fine as dust, glittered in the mid-morning sun. Satyabrata looked at her fondly before returning to the newspaper and his easy chair.

Satyabrata opened his eyes with a start. A low growl in his stomach told him that he was ravenous. He got up to see if Urmilla had fried any papads. He would enjoy them with his second cup of tea. Urmilla was nowhere in sight. The cup sat where he had left it.

Satyabrata was annoyed and a little puzzled too. Urmilla had never done this before.

'Where's your Maiji?' he asked the maid who was clearing up the utensils.

'Why dadababu, she has gone for her bath!'

Urmilla was usually the last person in the house to take a bath—her second in the day. She always took a shower early in the morning before entering the puja room. She bathed again after she had finished her chores, and the men had eaten their lunch. Then she ate along with Sonali. Satyabrata looked at the clock hanging over their dining table. It was two-thirty in the afternoon. He had overdone his pre-lunch siesta, but what annoyed him was no one had bothered to wake him up with a cup of tea, even though he had asked for it. He strode off to confront his wife.

'O go, what is this?' he said. 'Are you so busy nowadays that you can't serve your husband a cup of tea?'

Urmilla stood on the verandah bending slightly backwards. She had a gamchha clasped in her hands like a skipping rope, which she brought down with accuracy over the sheet of wet hair swinging down her back. Droplets of water splattered from her hair and hit Satyabrata full on the face. They felt like miniscule slaps on his cheeks. Satybrata's temper rose. He felt like shaking the water off from Urmilla's hair with his hands.

'Hanh go, aren't you going to answer me?' he cried irritably.

Urmilla stopped drying her hair and looked at him in surprise.

'What's the matter? Why are you shouting?'

'Why am I shouting she asks? Why am I shouting? It is already two-thirty. Have I been served my lunch? I asked for a cup of tea more than two hours ago! That cup is still lying where I left it in the kitchen!'

'Oh! Is that all? Well I was too busy cooking to see your cup. And since you were sleeping, I didn't want to disturb you.'

Urmilla went inside. Satyabrata followed her, feeling somewhat foolish. He didn't like creating scenes. But it had never been necessary in the past to express his wishes loudly. Perhaps his staying at home was making him too accessible. A man ought to maintain some distance from his family if he wanted respect. Satyabrata decided to go out of the house more often. But where?

There were not too many people of his age in their locality. They were either much older—senile! Or much younger—a bunch of louts! He could not loiter at the market because that would delay Urmilla's cooking. He could not go to the cinema all the time—too expensive. He would be better off watching TV.

But the last idea didn't turn out so well. There was one TV, around which everybody gathered in the evening. Since Debu and Shakti would be at work during the day, and the womenfolk would be busy with their chores, he could watch TV to his heart's content in the mornings. As it turned out, not only did the womenfolk watch TV, they were virtually addicted to the various serials shown at specific times. Sonali switched on the TV the minute Debu left for work, and whether she actually watched it or not, she sat on the sofa in front of it, idly flipping through the pages of a film magazine, getting up only to administer to the needs of her child, or to go to the bathroom. Sometimes she did get up for longer periods, but only when Urmilla requested her for help, that too in a sweet, cajoling voice. Sonali went slowly and grudgingly, grinding her rounded hips against the sofa as she got up to go. Satyabrata marvelled at how Urmilla's behaviour towards Sonali had changed. He had never before heard such dulcet notes, such coos and trills.

Urmilla enjoyed the same TV programmes as Sonali did so she often took a break to watch parts of them.

Satyabrata's year-old dadubhai had his own TV shows
to watch as well. That left only the evenings when Debu
and Shakti were home. They enjoyed the news and
sports channels, same as Satyabrata. But watching TV
in the evenings soon became a frustrating experience
for him. Satyabrata would just begin to get engrossed
in a particular programme when either Debu or Shakti
would switch to something else, and then back again.
So much channel switching made Satyabrata dizzy, but
nobody seemed to notice.

Satyabrata noticed. He noticed everything with
growing bitterness. The way they never bothered to
reply when he spoke, the way they ignored him when
he entered a room. Once Debu even cozied up to Sonali
in his presence, and that shameless hussy did not even
have the grace to blush!

As for Urmilla, she seemed to be on much better
terms with her daughter-in-law these days. Previously
she used to have some complaint or the other, and
Satyabrata would comfort her by saying that Sonali was
better than most girls of her generation. He would cite
examples, culled from the gossip that he had heard in
office. Besides, once Shakti brought home a wife, she
would be able to see Sonali's good points more clearly.
Urmilla would smile to herself whenever he made this
last observation. He had not understood at that time. But
after his retirement, and with Shakti's wedding almost

finalized, he believed he was just beginning to decipher
the meaning of her smile. Once Satyabrata even caught
her combing Sonali's hair, talking pleasantly about
this and that. Satyabrata found something distinctly
ingratiating in Urmilla's behaviour.

Satyabrata felt that the only person in the house who
would welcome him whole-heartedly was his dadubhai.
But even here he faced barriers. He discovered that
his little grandson, who could barely walk, followed a
strict regimen. He ate, bathed, slept, went for walks and
watched TV at specific times, which did not necessarily
match with Satyabrata's.

Satyabrata decided to go for long walks by himself.
He hoped that his prolonged absences would remind his
family that he was still the head of the family. 'Familiarity
breeds contempt,' quoted Satyabrata to himself. If the
womenfolk saw less of him during the day, they would
definitely start respecting him again. Initially, it seemed
to work. But one day, when Satyabrata returned home
much later than usual, he discovered that the whole
family had eaten: the table had been cleared and no one
had even bothered to keep a plate for him.

'I might as well be invisible!' thought Satyabrata
bitterly. Two salty tears rolled down his cheeks and on to
his dry, chapped lips. As Satyabrata licked them off, his
tongue encountered day-old stubble round the corners
of his mouth. He had forgotten to shave, and, of course,

Urmilla had not noticed. There was a time when she would complain softly and seductively when he forgot to shave, even after the children had grown up. But there was nothing nowadays.

Feeling humiliated and defeated, Satyabrata sat on the easy chair in the verandah. He thought of the money he had spent so freely on these turncoats. He thought of all the years of scrimping and saving to put his children through college and get his daughter and older son married. He thought of his wife and her diamond earrings. This was life. You worked like a slave when you were young so you could enjoy a bit of peace and respect in your old age, but from the moment of your superannuation you began to sink into oblivion. He buried his head in his hands to hide the tears…

~

Days passed. Satyabrata, feeling that nobody cared, did not bother with his appearance any more. He went about in shabby clothes, recycling and re-using his own and his sons' discarded shirts and pajamas… He took little interest in his meals, but took to raiding the kitchen whenever he felt hungry. Urmilla sometimes screamed at the maid or chased after an innocent stray cat. She did not notice even when he pilfered food from right under her nose. Once he even snatched a biscuit from his dadubhai's hands, just to see his reaction. But the child merely looked at his hands, and wriggled his chubby fingers. Satyabrata looked at his grandson for a long time, and then, ashamed of himself, returned the biscuit to the still wriggling fingers.

One day, Satyabrata decided to pay his office a visit. His ex-colleagues may not have time for him, but surely the canteen boys at the cafeteria he used to frequent during lunchtime, the owner of the paan-shop where he bought his sachet of Pan Parag, and Manoj would remember him? He would enjoy listening to some real gossip.

Satyabrata swung his black umbrella as he walked along the road. He almost believed that he was a gainfully employed man once again. The old landmarks, the potholes on the road, the faces of the bus conductors, shop owners and even many of the pedestrians seemed so familiar and welcoming that Satyabrata couldn't stop smiling at all and sundry. That nobody returned his smiles did not bother Satyabrata. He had not come this way for so long, how could he blame them? Soon Satyabrata came to the pipal tree under which a barber set up his open-air shop every day. Most of the office peons had their beards shaved here. Satyabrata knew the barber by face. He had often nodded at him, though he had never taken up the barber's offer of a haircut and shave. Satyabrata rubbed his chin. Maybe he would surprise the old boy today. Just then Satyabrata spied Manoj, walking less than three feet away from him.

'Ki re Manoj?' he hailed. 'How's work going? How are the babus treating you?'

Manoj did not answer. He hurried down the road, carrying a bundle of letters with a busy man's worried expression on his face. Satyabrata's face reddened at this slight. How dare Manoj ignore him, that ungrateful wretch!

'Did you see that?' he said to the barber. The barber smiled ingratiatingly. 'What are you smiling about, you oaf!'

But the barber went on smiling and nodding his head. He did not seem to have heard Satyabrata at all. Satyabrata felt worse. Now a roadside barber, who would have been overcome with pride in the past if Satyabrata had patronized him, was ignoring him. Anger welled up and almost choked him. Satyabrata wanted to throttle the barber and smash the mirror on Manoj's head. He spat viciously on the road as he turned to go.

Just then, his eyes fell on the glass window of an electronics showroom. Reflected in it, he saw people around him going about their daily business. He saw the barber smiling ingratiatingly at a potential customer who did not want a shave and was shaking his head vigorously to get this point across. He saw a couple of his ex-colleagues who had probably gone out to have a private conversation on the pretext of a cup of tea. He saw a lady diffidently looking at a washing machine inside the shop. Satyabrata saw the whole world around him reflected in the glass. This used to be his world, too, before retirement. But his own reflection was missing. His curiosity roused, Satyabrata peered into the glass for a closer look. Nothing.

Satyabrata stood very still, digesting this discovery. He could no longer hear the noise of the traffic and the people around him. He tried to catch a glimpse of himself from every possible angle but could find no reflection. He felt panic rise in his breast; his heart fluttered wildly. Satyabrata turned around and looked into the barber's mirror. The mirror gazed blankly back at him. He picked it up and peered closely. The shadows cast by the swaying leaves of the pipal tree and portions of an office building were visible. But his face was not, even when he held the mirror right up to his nose.

Satyabrata almost lost his balance. Was it true then? Had he indeed vanished? Just to make sure, Satyabrata made a face at the gentleman standing directly in his path. It was a deliberate action and Satyabrata made certain they were face to face. The man did not react. Satyabrata made a face again. Still no reaction. The man stared ahead as if there was no one standing in front of him, and nothing had happened.

Reeling from the shock of the discovery, Satyabrata walked unsteadily to a patch of muddy grass between two intersecting streets. It was meant to be a small park, but was so badly maintained that nobody used it, except for beggars and rickshaw pullers. Satyabrata sat down heavily on a bit of still-wet grass. He looked around him. He had vanished from this world. Nobody could see or hear him. He repeated this to himself a number of times.

As he sat there thinking about his life after retirement, Satyabrata became more and more convinced that he had not disappeared happened overnight; he must have been vanishing layer by layer, like a neglected oil painting. As Satyabrata mused over his life he felt himself moving away like a man who has just disembarked and is watching the train pull out from the station. He leaned into the grass and breathed deeply. His anger and outrage began to melt away. He tilted his head skyward and returned the sky's hard glare without flinching. He had actually, completely vanished.

The hilarity of his situation struck him like a bolt. Now he could do whatever he liked. He could do anything and get away with it. He need not bother about what people would say or think, least of all his own family. Now he was free, truly free! Satyabrata Chatterjee stood up and to laugh. He guffawed with his head thrown back, his arms akimbo. He laughed as he had never laughed before.

Mail for Dadubhai

28th September, 11:30:15 AM

Dear, dear Dadubhai,

Surprised? What you were thinking? Your Dadu is old man? Your Dadu may be old, but he is still learning new tricks. He is learning internet letter writing! So he can send letters at any time! Even when you are sleeping; just now you are sleeping, no? It is now mid-morning in Kolkata, so in New Jersey it is how much time? I am calculating it is now 2 a.m. You are in deep sleep now Dadubhai. But your Dadu is thinking of you and wishing you sweet dreams. These dreams are travelling very fast via computers, entering your room and blessing you.

Dadubhai, please note Indian Standard Time in my email. I am wanting that you know at what time I am writing. The exact Indian time; and then you can match it with your watch. Are you still wearing your Mickey Mouse watch?

Goodnight, my Dadubhai.

Dadu

~

28th September, 11:45:10 PM

Dear, dear Dadubhai,

It is still today, but I am writing again. Now it is also your today. So we are sharing one today. Only my today is ending, like my life, but your today is starting, like your life. Even so at one point we are sharing that life! How wonderful God's timing is, no? It must be now lunch time there in New Jersey. Here I have finished dinner. Your Thammu is already sleeping. Do you know your Thammu is nowadays snoring? Very softly, but she is snoring. Don't tell her I am telling you her secret.

I am remembering the secret we used to keep when you were two years of age. You won't remember it. But in my mind it is fresh like yesterday. Your mother said no sweets for you. 'No, no!' she said. Your mother is very particular. Only imported, American baby food for you. But I am giving you Bengali sweet, one small piece sandesh and one small piece rosogullah. Aah! Dadubhai, your face became so bright, like the full moon. You were saying, 'Mmmmm. Dadadada!' So in secret I was giving you sweet. And, you were keeping my secret. Do you remember the sandesh your Thammu was making for you from tin milk when we went to New Jersey? You were four years old at that time. Now you are big boy. You are studying now in what class? I am thinking you are in class nine, because you will be fourteen years old on October 31st. Am I correct? Nine is senior class. I am hoping you will write when you get time.

Good morning Dadubhai.

Dadu

~

1st October, 11:20:13 AM

Dear, dear Dadubhai,

I am missing you very much. Old age is cud-chewing age. But I don't only want to chew my memories. I want to enjoy the Pujas with my only grandson. It is selfish of me. So don't mind it. Your Thammu and I are always seeing the photographs. But heart is not satisfied. You are young, busy with your life. We know. Enjoy your life, dadubhai. Young age is time for doing and doing. That is how you will grow big. And we will be so proud of you.

Dadu

~

3rd October, 7:03:15 PM

Hi Dadu,

Sorry I couldn't write earlier. You're right, it's busy here. I go for practice early in the mornings. Then it's back home for breakfast, then school, and after that back home again, homework, assignments, dinner, and so on. On Sundays I attend Bengali classes at the Bengali People's Club or association if you like. I have to. It's a rule in this house. Btw, I'm in high school. Grade 9 is high school here.

Cool you're learning email dadu. Way to go! But who's teaching you?

I don't recall that sweet-eating incident. I was two, right? Do you know any more stories about me? I sort of recall your stay with us at the old place. Now we live in another house with a bigger yard and a pool. One time I got lost in some market in Kolkata—can't remember the name. I think I was about six or seven then. I got nightmares about it for a long time. Now, of course I'm too old to lose my way.

Dadu, I don't wear a Mickey Mouse watch any more. Dad got me a nice one this time. Some of my friends have real cool watches. Better than mine.

Ok, g2g. Love to Thammu (does she really snore?!) and you.

Neil

~

4th October, 11: 12:10 AM
Dear, dear Dadubhai,

Hi! Oh what a surprise! I am so happy. But why you are writing Neil? You have such a beautiful name—Neelanjan. Why you are making it so small, spelling is also different? Your home name is Manik. Are you knowing that Manik means jewel? You can use that one, it is short. But never mind. Your friends are perhaps not able to say Neelanjan, so you are cutting it into Neel. Do you know of one very famous American who was also called Neel? He is Neel Armstrong. The first man on the moon. He said, 'One small step for a man. One giant step for mankind.' Your Baba was a small boy at that time. It was 1969. I remember it.

Yes, I remember losing you in New Market. You were six. Your Thammu and I were doing birthday shopping for you. Your parents were having some other programme that day. One second I turned, and you vanished. I almost had heart attack. Luckily one shopkeeper spotted you and picked you up. He made you stand up on shop counter and shout. Big crowd gathered. When we found you, all the shopkeepers scolded us. I still have nightmares about that day, Dadubhai. But here in Kolkata, there are still good people living. That is why you were found.

Dadubhai, I cannot write you a long letter today as I have hospital appointment. Don't worry. These are only old age problems. I will write to you when I come back.

Your Thammu is sending her heart full of love. And, also saying Hi!

Dadu

~

6th October, 7:08:30 AM

Dear, dear Dadubhai,

Hi! Yesterday, I was wanting to write to you as soon as I came back from doctor. He made me do many tests, blood test, urine test, what not. Anyhow, I came home tired but determined to write to you. But there was power cut. Nowadays, Kolkata is not getting power cuts at all, unlike many years ago, when your Baba was a student here, but yesterday our building cable had problem. So, no power. But today it is coming back and I am immediately writing. Your Thammu who is doing her prayers is laughing at me. She is saying I have got new toy to play with in retirement. I am saying this is not toy. Computer is my private postman for Dadubhai!

Perhaps you are thinking, what this Dadu is doing? Has he no work? Always writing? But, I am new student of computer and internet. I am wanting to practice much. Even now I am not good. I am making many mistakes. Chinmoy is correcting me. Chinmoy is helping me learn internet; it is Chinmoy who selected the right computer after your father sent money. You may be wondering who is this Chinmoy? Chinmoy is your Dadu's cousin sister's brother-in-law's son's son. Oh, my God what a long relation! Are you confused? Here in Kolkata, we are making brother and sister out of our neighbours and grandchildren out of their grandchildren. But not to worry, Dadubhai. Nobody is taking your place. You are my only Dadubhai. Chinmoy is like grandson, but he is not you. He is coming to Kolkata all the way from small town in Malda district, because he is wanting to study more. Dadubhai, I am having high hopes for your studies. Are you knowing your father was first boy in class? That is why he is doing big job in America. For many years India was facing brain drain. All our best brains were going to America. But now they are also coming back. Now India is also doing good. Delhi, Bombay, Madras, Bangalore, all these are like foreign countries now. I have not seen with my own eyes, for I am old man. I am all the time reading in paper. But Kolkata is still a very loving place. Here if you are sick or needy, everybody is helping. Like Chinmoy. He is telling me, Bhalo-dadu, (that is what he is calling me, Bhalo-dadu or in English, Good Dadu!) why you are not learning internet? Come, I will show you. It is nothing. Your Dadubhai in New Jersey will be so happy to get email from you. Your son will be so proud. So he is teaching me; slowly, slowly I am picking up, first typing then surfing, reading mails, copy-paste, spelling check—my English is not like yours, it is Benglish! No?

Anyhow, I have now written for very long time, and my hand is paining. Chinmoy is sending you his greetings. He is going to college. It is good we have

Chinmoy with us, two old people. I think Chinmoy is also happy to be here.

God Bless you, my Dadubhai.

Dadu

~

8th October, 4:10:10 PM

Dear, dear Dadubhai,

Hi! I am having small fever. That is why no letter yesterday. But not to worry. I am fine. It is only small sickness. Don't tell Baba, he will worry. After getting better, I am opening email. I am thinking maybe there is a surprise, but my inbox is empty.

Dadubhai, your motherland is so beautiful now. I wish you were here. It is Sarat Kaal or Fall, as you say in America. For us this season begins from end of September or beginning of October. Durga Puja festival is less than fifteen days away. Air is now slightly cold, like your summer time. Sky is clear with only few white fluffy clouds. They look like rabbits. Do you know your father was keeping rabbits? They were white with red eyes. They knew their names. Oh! How much he cried when the rabbits died. Your father fell sick. Then he got better and said, 'Baba, I will be doctor when I grow up. I will heal peoples and animals. No one will die.' And, your father is keeping promise. He was studying so hard, and then he was getting scholarship to study

in England and become doctor. After that he returned
and practiced in Kolkata. Then again he went, this time
to America. Now you are all settled there. I know your
father and mother are missing Kolkata now. They had
spent childhood here. No Bengali likes to be away from
motherland during Durga Puja. This is the season when
Bengal becomes as beautiful as a new bride. The white
Kaash flowers are swaying in the fields like swan feathers.
The Shiuli flowers are filling up air with sweet scent.
They are falling like white carpet on the grass. Every
morning your Thammu is picking up the flowers for her
prayers. The Dhakias are drumming their dhaks—you
know? These are the drums and drummers of Bengal.
They come every Durga Puja. All families are visiting
their relatives. Everybody is buying new clothes. But we
cannot buy for you because you are far away. So I am
writing letter to your father to buy new clothes for you
and your mother on our behalf. I think New Jersey is
having large Bengali community. You will see the Puja
there, no?

Tomorrow we are going to Gariahat market to buy
new clothes for Chinmoy. He is saying, 'No. No. Bhalo-
dadu don't buy for me.' But we are saying, 'Chhi, chhi.
How can you say so? Of course we will buy new clothes
for you. You are away from your parents. We are like
your grandparents.' Then he is accepting. So tomorrow,
three of us will hire a taxi and go. Your Thammu is very

happy. She will eat lunch outside. No cooking. Tomorrow is holiday for her.

Is your mother getting any holiday? I know you cannot get maid servant in America. She must be getting tired. Are you helping her?

I will write again Dadubhai. Take our love.

Dadu

~

8th October, 07:01:30 PM

Hi Dadu,

Sorry about your illness. Please get better. I didn't tell Dad, because you told me not to. I heard him telling Mom that he'll call you sometime during the festival. So, we'll get to talk.

Yeah, I got new clothes and stuff. But I won't wear them now. Mom wants me to wear them for the Pujas. We'll be going to the Bengali Puja here. Mom and her friends are really excited; they are busy cooking things, doing stuff. They wanted me to do a recitation, but I've got too many school projects. We'll attend the shows in the evenings. G2g Dadu. Get better, I mean that. Loved the rabbit story about Dad! ☺

Btw Neil is easy to pronounce. My friends and teachers were murdering Neelanjan. Nobody calls me Manik here!

Neil

PS: Dadu, can you collect pictures for me about Durga Puja and other Bengali celebrations? Got a project on the subject. Say Hi to Thammu!

~

10th October, 5:30:11 AM
My dear, dear Dadubhai,

Hi! I am so sorry my reply is late. Are you thinking this Dadu has forgotten you? No, no. The sun can rise from the west and fishes fly in the sky, but this Dadu's heart is always full of love for his Dadubhai. ☺ See? I am also learning smiley icon. Chinmoy is teaching me. He is also teaching me grumpy icon: ☹ But I am not needing that icon—only smiley for my Dadubhai! We Bengalis are very sentimental people. We love and cry easily. We also love to eat. This is the season for Bengali delicacies. Your Thammu is preparing nice sweets and fish dishes. Chinmoy is enjoying. I am also enjoying. But we are also feeling sad; we are thinking what you, your father and mother are eating there in America. We know you are not getting fresh pabda and tangra fish. We know you are not getting our special Bengali vegetables. Anyhow, let me know what Bengali food you are eating.

Durga Puja is starting some days later. But Kolkata's roads are already crowded and colourful. It is not good for me to go out now. So Chinmoy is helping us by doing all vegetable and fish shopping. He is taking your

Thammu to the market and carrying her bags. He is getting up very early to match your Thammu's timing. I am also rising early. I am writing early morning letter to you.

I also collecting pictures and Chinmoy is loading them into computer. He will make attachment and mail to you, because I am still not expert. I still don't understand how to operate the scanning and printing machine. But I am learning. I am not giving up. Today Chinmoy is there. Tomorrow he will pass out, take job and go to another place. Then who will help me? I have to be self-dependent. The first Prime Minister of our country, Sri Jawaharlal Nehru said that India must be self-sufficient. That was Gandhiji's words also. Is your mother and father teaching you about India? I hope so. You must love America because you are American citizen. But you must also love your history and your culture. Old Indians like your Thammu and me, ask for nothing else in return.

Today, I have written marathon letter to you. Your Thammu and Chinmoy have come back from market and your Thammu has finished making breakfast. You may be wondering, how so? Dadubhai, my fingers are not moving as fast as yours or Chinmoy's! I am taking double time for every word I am writing.

Today also, I am feeling more tired. Maybe because my night sleep was not good. But not to worry. After breakfast, I will be better. Your Thammu is calling me now. So I will take your leave.

Thammu and I shower our blessings on you.

Dadu

~

13th October, 09:30:33 PM

Dear Neel,

Your Dadu was taken ill day before yesterday. We admitted him to the nursing home. He has suffered a stroke. We were tensed because this happened during the Puja time. But we made it on time and your Dadu got the doctor's attention duly. Now he is still in ICU. However, I think Ma Durga is smiling on him. So we are hopeful. Your Thammu is being strong. But of course family is family. I have telephoned your father. I will go to receive you at the airport. Not to worry. Your Dadu was in his senses when we took him to hospital. That time, although he was finding some difficulty talking, he told me to scan the pictures he had collected and email them to you. They are in the attachment.

My regards to your parents,

Chinmoy dada

~

13th October 1.30 AM

Respected Chinmoy dada,

Thank you for taking care of my Dadu. Tell Dadu and Thammu that I am coming too. Tell Dadu that I want to light the Diwali lamps with him. So he has to get well soon. Tell Thammu that I am looking forward to eating her cooking. Please tell them. And give them both my love.

See you at the airport on Tuesday.

Yours,

Neel/Manik

~

15th October, 10 PM

Dear little brother Neel,

I read your letter aloud to your Dadu today. Your Thammu was crying beside his bed. But your Dadu's face was serene. His eyes were closed, as if he was listening very attentively. Be strong for your Thammu. Blood is blood. You may not know it, but you are the only one who can bring a smile in this house. There is a saying in Bengali that the interest is more valuable than the capital. Meaning that grandson is more valuable than son! Do not be too worried. I will go to the airport to receive you as I promised.

Blessings and heart full with love from your Dadu and Thammu.

Your

Chinmoy Dada.

Old Man Sitting on a South Kolkata Park Bench, Ruminating

See that young girl wearing jeans? She is having two fully grown bosoms that are jutting out like very ripe mangoes. No shame she has, wearing tight T-shirt. These days all the girls are like that. I am wondering: What kind of daughter-in-law will she make? Certainly not like my very own daughter-in-law.

I remember when she first came into our house, how she bent down to touch my feet. Her blouse was a low-cutting blouse, only little, after all she was a decent girl from good family—her parents did not create problems with our demands for the marriage. They smilingly took our list and did not try to cut down. Mind you, we were not asking for dowry. No. Not at all. We were only giving them the list of gifts be given to our family members and what they should do to be most hospitable to us during the marriage ceremony. We did not utter a word about money or gold or anything like that. We are also very decent family and our son is doing a very good job in a computer company. Yes, he has been to foreign countries also, for training-shaining. My daughter-in-law's father and mother behaved well. Even though we did not demand, they gave decent gold jewellery and good saris and utensils and furniture to their daughter, plus good saris to all our female relatives and dhotis to the men. They provided good food and good hotel accommodation. We also took good care of them when they came for the reception. Of course being the boy's side, we are not obliged, but because we are cultured we were very hospitable to them. Even afterwards when my daughter-in-law's family used to come, my wife would prepare very good food. My daughter-in-law also helped her in the kitchen.

I was having no complains. A young, fresh-like-a-morning-flower woman was in my house, and she was being most respectful to me. She was bending down to touch my feet and I could see her mangoes. Yes, she was always giving me many opportunities to see, because she was so respectful. I was giving her my full affection, almost like a father, but my better half was getting angry. She started finding many faults with daughter-in-law's cooking. So just to make her more and more angry I used to ask for second helping. So daughter-in-law was giving me; she was bending, her head covered, and ladling the food into my plate. Oh what a fun it was to see two women fighting for my attention.

After two years when grandson came, I would be

passing by with my head bent, but from under my spectacles I was seeing how much in full bloom my daughter-in-law had grown; motherhood had made her full to overflowing with beauty. Sometimes her sari was getting wet with milk. What sweet milk it must have been. The honey smell of new milk was around her all the time. One day she even forgot to button her blouse! Ah! I felt like taking out my dentures immediately and putting my mouth there. The last stage of man is back to being a baby, so my needs were nothing but a natural outcome of time. Nevertheless I controlled my desire and asked her for tea instead. She immediately went into the kitchen and made me hot sweet tea. She is a good daughter-in-law. I was happy with her. But my wife was jealous. Women are always jealous of each other. That is their nature. Men should be strict with the women. But nowadays men are losing their manliness in front of their women. This country is going to the dogs.

Now my son and daughter-in-law are living apart from us. They have bought a smart and brand new apartment at the far end of Kolkata, where all these big big IT firms are coming up. I have heard that this part of Kolkata is the latest posh locality. Nowadays Ballygunge and Gol Park are shabby old places. My son is also having brand new Ford car. It is a very big car. All this is very fine. I want my son to succeed. But why live so far away?

But I am not the only one. All my friends are in the

same problem. At least my son is still in Kolkata. Others are having NRI children. They are proud, but very sad also. This habit of staying away from parents was not there in our time. You will say that our old traditions are breaking. But I say that women cannot tolerate one another. Yes, that is the real trouble these days. Mother-in-law and daughter-in-law always fighting, like cats. Everywhere you go, this is the same story. Women are like that only, but nowadays the men have become weak. No control over family.

What is happening is happening. The world is changing. But I am missing my grandson. That will never change. Previously, every morning I would take him with me when I went for morning walk. That time he was just a six-month-old baby. I was free to show my friends that indeed I was proud grandfather of a boy. I would open his pant to show them. My friends would kiss him in the soft manly part. I was also kissing him. But one day my son saw, luckily not me doing it, but my friend, and he was getting very angry. 'Why you have allowed your friend to do this nefarious activity!' he was saying many times. Nefarious activity? What new thing is this? I am his grandfather, how can I do anything nefarious to my grandson? My ear drums were bursting. My pressure was going up. My wife was not able to make him understand that in our generation this is done. It is also a custom to take a picture with your naked grandson on your lap so that the whole world can see the permanent record of your son's son, and how your seed lives on from generation to generation. My father also had one of my son. The framed pictures used to hang on a wall in his room where he could see from his bed. It is very normal. You must be proud of your grandson's manly part. You must show to the world that your son is capable of giving birth to a son. But these days they are having too many ideas in their heads. They are going against tradition and all the things we were proud of.

Now they are living in a separate house. Sometimes they are inviting us. Like guests. Yes, I have become a guest in my own son's house. My wife and I are going and sitting in the drawing room. Daughter-in-law is serving food and we are playing with grandson under her supervision. They are buying presents for us. But what is the use of all these things? I am only wanting my grandson. Now that he is older, of course I will not need to show his manly part. Of course neither my friends nor I are going to kiss or fondle him there. That requirement is over. But I am still active. I could have taken him to school. I could have taken him to park. I could have told him so many stories from my childhood. This is how our history and culture is passed on; from grandfather to grandchild. But who listens to an old man?

Nowadays I am doing my morning walk up to this park every day. Then, I am sitting here and watching traffic and people. Sometimes my friends are joining me. But today I am alone with my thoughts and that girl's mangoes. And also her vanity bag. I am observing these days girls and women are carrying vanity bags of many styles. They are also keeping many things inside the bags. Sometimes I am thinking that girls and women are keeping their whole possessions inside of their vanity bags. We, the manly type men, are not like that. Only one wallet, and for going to office one portmanteau bag. The portmanteau bag for keeping important files and tiffin box. It was also safe place for bringing home pencils, rubbers, pens and other small stationery items from office. Children were small at that time, why to waste money on buying school stationeries? So I was bringing home these things. This was normal practice, open secret. It was part of our undeclared salary in those days. But these days the companies are not giving anything to their loyal employees. My son is telling that it is all cost to company. The company is only seeing how much you are costing inclusive of perks. I cannot imagine how much these modern companies would have charged me for my pencils and rubbers. I am understanding fully well how difficult life is nowadays. But mind it, we are also having some more comforts. The TV channels are many and so there is entertainment choice. And everything is colour. I am liking my news channel and National Geographic the most. The Discovery channel and History channel are also very good. My wife is watching only Bengali tele-serials. I am not complaining as long as she is keeping her mouth shut. Only problem is when there is cricket match.

After so many years of being married to a man, why she is not knowing what cricket is to us? I am absolutely not understanding. But modern-day girls are little bit more understanding. I am sitting here on my park bench and hearing young school-girl type girls talking about how handsome Dhoni is and how cute Sehwag is. I don't know how much cricket they are understanding but they are at least not creating trouble for us men by wanting to see telly-serial during match time. Nowadays our own Saurabh, our Bengal's gaurob, is not taking centre stage. But he is still the big dada of Indian cricket. I am blessing him many times in my heart. Our Saurabh is the only Bengali standing who is bringing self-respect to our land.

O what a land Bengal was. What do these young people know? They are knowing nothing. They have not seen the tiger Bengal. They have no idea what Bengal was in British times. Capital of India! They are not knowing that the best industries were here. The best artists. The best writers. Best singers. They are only knowing Rabindranath Tagore and Satyajit Ray. That is very good. But Bengal was having so many other luminaries also. In all the fields. Ah, but what is use? What is the use in thinking of past glorious days? Now Bengal is tiger without any teeth. Just like me. I am needing false teeth to chew fish and rice. I cannot eat corn. I cannot eat guava. The monsoon is coming but bringing me no joy.

There was a time when I was stopping at one particular Bihari man's trolley to buy tender corn cob which he was then roasting on a small portable unoon with hot coals in it and he was fanning it to keep the coals from burning out, and the light green leaves of the cobs were in a soft pile on the wet road. A cow or two would munch on the waste. The unpeeled cobs would be piled on his trolley on one side and the unoon at the other end and yellow lemon pieces on enamel plate and rock salt in a jar in between. I remember the smell of the tender cobs roasting and the blue smoke rising. Right next to him would be the guava woman, sitting on her haunches with her basket of fresh green guavas and also some rock salt in a jar. I would be buying four or five guavas and asking her to slice one. She would be cutting it neatly and sprinkling rock salt on the wedges and then putting the lot on a sal leaf. After this all I would be needing was a hot cup of tea, but for that I had to wade through calf-length dirty water for the gullies of Ballygunge were having poor drainage; yes, even today there is water-logging all over Kolkata.

Now that life is gone. That house in Ballygunge is sold to builders for tall apartment building in which I am owning one flat but I am not staying there. I am giving it on rent because the prices of necessities are going up so high that I am constantly needy. Now that my son has moved away, he does not think he should look after this old father of his who worked so hard to send him to good school and engineering college. I don't know why in this country we are so son-crazy. Everywhere I see the daughters are more dutiful. The sons always follow their wives. But I must not say bad things about my daughter-in-law. Initially she was a good daughter-in-law. My wife is no saint, but I have to defend her. I have also grown old. My teeth for cracking walnuts are gone. Sometimes I am thinking it is better for me to suck milk from a bottle. Better it would be if I could suck it from a woman's breasts. I would love to become baby once more, no responsibilities, and everybody loving me.

My wife's breasts are dry. Besides she will be shocked if I make my desire known to her. She will think I am indecent man. Why are women so difficult? I have seen how slowly and slowly she has pushed me away after the children were born. Even night time for me was a duty for her. Are they not having any desire? But as soon as daughter-in-law is inside the house, they are feeling insecure. I was still prepared after retirement to satisfy her. But she was not liking it so much. I could tell. What is the use? I could have spent money…at least such type of women would have pretended to like me.

Of course I have never visited those types of places, ever. My colleague Ghanshyam Das has. But I am a man of very good character. I will never betray my own lawfully wedded wife. Looking at mangoes does not mean I am climbing the tree and stealing them. Anyway now I have to go home as the sun is very hot. I will drink a cup of tea made by Dipta, our new maid. Now that my wife is having many arthritic pains and other female ailments, we are keeping this girl. She is a young girl who has come from Diamond Harbour to earn money in a respectable way in Kolkata. I am happy to give her shelter. And she is very respectful to me.

Acknowledgements

My sincere thanks to my editors at Speaking Tiger—Anurag Basnet and Shalini Krishan. Gratitude to the editors of the journals where some of the stories have appeared in some guise or another. And, my spouse and children—everything I do, I do for you.